Brothers for Life

Brothers
for
Life

Keith W. Wander

CROSSWAY BOOKS • WHEATON, ILLINOIS
A DIVISION OF GOOD NEWS PUBLISHERS

Brothers for Life.

Copyright © 1991 by Keith W. Wander.

Published by Crossway Books, a division of
Good News Publishers, 1300 Crescent St., Wheaton, Illinois 60187.

Cover illustration: David Yorke

First printing, 1991

Printed in the United States of America

Library of Congress Cataloging-in-Publication Data
Wander, Keith W., 1941-
    Brothers for life / Keith W. Wander.
      p.   cm.
    I. Title.
PS3573.A4768B76 1991   813'.54—dc20   91-3260
ISBN 0-89107-621-2

99	98	97	96	95	94	93	92	91
15	14	13	12	11	10	9	8	7	6	5	4	3	2	1

For
Roger Allen Wander
September 23, 1944 – January 5, 1985
my brother for life

Do you not know that if you yield yourselves to anyone
as obedient slaves, you are slaves of the one whom you
obey, either of sin, which leads to death,
or of obedience, which leads to righteousness? But thanks
be to God, that you who were once slaves of sin
have become obedient from the heart to the standard
of teaching to which you were committed, and,
having been set free from sin, have become
slaves of righteousness.

ROMANS 6:16-18 (RSV)

PART I

ONE

Next to Jesus Christ, I thought of Barry Gieselmann as the most gifted and talented person who ever walked the face of this earth. I don't mean to sound sacrilegious; God knows better than anyone that I have tried to serve and worship Him to the best of my ability for the past twenty years.

With Barry, however, it was not so much a reverence I had for him as it was an awe of his abilities, both physical and mental. He was one of the few people I had ever met who could say he was going to develop a new skill and then begin to master it almost immediately. He never said it in a boastful way, or with false humility, but simply declared he would do something and then proceeded to get it accomplished. I've counseled many people who found themselves locked into jobs they hated—or even worse, ended up hating themselves. Barry would not be the kind of person who would ever fall into that dilemma. He had the uncanny knack of thinking about a subject for a while, then simply acting any way he felt moved about the matter.

One day he had been reading about great artists and was especially impressed by Gauguin's water colors. Without hesitation he declared he would take up painting. We had lived together for less than a year at the time, and I couldn't tell if he was teasing or serious. The next afternoon I entered the room to find him asleep. Beside his plain brown, metal-framed bed was an easel with an oil portrait of a beautiful, black-haired woman holding a bunch of pale green grapes beneath the jawline of her tanned cheeks. Her hazel eyes had a distant stare, and she seemed not to notice her creator lying in a bed, no longer attracted to her silent charms. Or was he spent from trying to win her over and could not persuade her that someone as beautiful as she could be happy with him, an itinerant student who had missed all of that morning's classes in an effort to know her better? In any case she was beautiful, and it was obvious from the paint stains on his T-shirt Barry had brought her into this world through the strokes of his brushes. I woke him at dinner time and began to chatter away at the wonder he had performed on canvas.

He didn't say anything in return to my compliments, but walked to his dresser and pulled out a paper-covered book almost as big as the painting he had just completed. It was a "how to" on painting portraits. He had read it from cover to cover, marking certain sections filled with illustrations of noses, lips, and eyes. A page from a magazine floated out of the book onto the floor. I picked it up and found the same woman who was on the canvas. Barry had not only duplicated the picture—he made it even more alive by adding texture, color, and light the photographer had probably captured but which was lost in the printing of the magazine. To me it was a marvel, a flash of brilliance, the quickest study I had ever seen by one person in the twenty years of my life. He merely grunted as he dressed in the clothes he had strewn around the room the night before. Impervious to my compliments and congratulations, he scratched at his belly and yawned while I continued to yammer away at how wonderful his artwork was. Finally I could stand his indifference no longer.

"Aren't you the least bit excited about how good this is?" I asked as I held the painting in front of me.

"Roomie," he said flatly, "the difference between goodness and greatness is as far as east is from west." With that, he walked out of the room. And to the best of my knowledge he never picked up a paintbrush again.

That's the way it was with him. He was so good at everything and made it look so easy, people like me could have easily developed an inferiority complex being around him—except nothing he did seemed to impress *him* as much as it did the rest of us. One Saturday when a group of us were looking for something to do other than study or watch reruns of game shows on television, one of the guys in the house suggested we play golf at a public course. On that particular day Barry shot a 37 for nine holes because he "couldn't putt." The next closest score was Lyle's, a guy from across the hall, with a 55. Lyle had a 55 because he couldn't putt, drive, or chip, but could lie better than any of us as we recorded our strokes. Lyle's real score was probably 75, and we all knew it; only Lyle believed he was within eighteen strokes of Barry's score. On that day I learned Barry had been a 4 handicap golfer but rarely played, and almost never practiced even when he did play because it "got too hot in the summer."

The only skill I ever saw him practice was playing the piano. Barry would sit for hours on end playing classical pieces from Rachmaninoff, Chopin, Bach, and Beethoven. We had an old upright piano at the house where we lived, but most of the residents complained if he practiced there. He knew every piano on the campus, however, and would sometimes practice until 4 A.M., with no awareness of the time or energy he had spent at the keyboard. And the music he played was remarkable. It was more a series of passions, flights of fancy, or reveries than an arrangement of notes. People who happened by the places where he practiced never complained as the residents of our house did. Instead, they sat down and listened with wonderment as he played with an intensity almost as fascinating to me as the music itself. He did not look the role of the stereotypical classical musician. His hair was short, and his body was muscular. In many ways he resembled Mickey Mantle, right down to the chiseled grin marks on his cheeks. When he smiled or was in deep concentration, he could squint his eyes in such a way that I could never be sure if he could see or not. His eyeballs seemed to be swallowed up by eyelids and cheeks, with only hairline slits displayed where his eyes had once been. When he played the piano, he would squint his eyes and move his arms so the muscles in his forearms rippled as he moved his fingers across the keyboard. His fingers were not delicate, but large and strong, on hands that would appear to be more at home on the handle of an axe than on an ivory keyboard.

After a long study session one evening, we went over to the commons area where students lounged at all hours of the night. It was nearly 1 A.M. when he began to play. After two or three short pieces he launched into Rachmaninoff's "Theme from Romeo and Juliet." To tell the truth, I didn't know that's what it was called at the time. Today they run these very snobby ads on television suggesting you aren't really cultured if you can't recognize the song in three or four bars. Every time I see the ad, it brings me back to that night in the commons. People began to gather around him as he played. His arms flexed, fingers flew, and he physically attacked the keyboard with his whole body by lifting himself off the piano bench during certain sections of the song. The only way I knew for sure his eyes were open was when he looked at his hands, first one hand, then the other, as he encountered difficult passages in the bass or treble clef. I generally don't acknowledge much emotion in my life, but that evening chills ran up my spine. I had never seen anyone so devoted, so absorbed in his work, and have the work sound so beautiful and compelling.

When he finished, about twenty people had gathered, and they broke into spontaneous applause. I, too, clapped like mad, and tears welled in my eyes. To this day I don't know why. It was just a moving moment in my life, and I was proud to even know Barry, let alone be his roommate. He barely recognized the applause, but simply nodded his head a few times to those who were clapping and patting him on the back. On the way back to the house I told him how perfectly I thought he had done. Instead of acknowledging my compliments he said, "I made three mistakes. But then you don't need Gieselmann if you're going to record over the mistakes." This was a cryptic comment he liked to make, attributed to Vladimir Horowitz. The Russian pianist was told by a recording studio to play part of a concerto again so they could dub over the one mistake he had made. Horowitz told them they didn't need him to play anything at all if they were going to record over the mistakes, and he walked off.

I don't want to suggest Barry was some kind of stuffed shirt who couldn't have fun. Because he played the piano so beautifully, people were always bringing him sheet music they would like him to play during his practices. I personally had given him a copy of Gershwin's "Rhapsody in Blue," and he started out sight-reading it with more difficulty than I thought he might have. After five minutes or so he broke into a boogie-woogie, smiled a toothy grin, turning his eyes into slits, and said, "You can always tell a Gershwin tune." More boogie-woogie for two minutes, then he said, "Gimme some a dat greasy chicken." Just as quickly he was back into Gershwin's syncopated rhythms. I thought he was funny, witty, and charming in an offbeat kind of way. Many others thought he was eccentric at best and in all probability a little crazy. He would go on strange diets based on his own reasoning about nutrition. For one entire week he ate nothing but chocolate donuts with chocolate icing washed down with quarts of chocolate milk. The entire next week he drank only bouillon broth followed by a week of beer and Snickers bars, ending the month with a week of meat and potatoes.

Perhaps the one habit setting him apart from everyone was that he almost never dated an American girl. He had an attraction for foreign women, or at least those who had foreign parents and maintained the look of someone who might be an immigrant. Some of the guys teased him about it, and the coeds who showed an interest in him resented it, but the opinions of others didn't seem to bother him one way or the other. We talked about it once, and it was clear he didn't want to discuss it in any depth. The only thing he did say was, "I don't have to put as much energy into foreign women as it takes with Americans. At the end of an evening with an American woman I know I've had a bad time if it feels like my face is going to break from the fake smile I've had on for the past two hours." End of conversation. We never talked about it again. We double-dated many times, and each time he was with a Japanese, Indian, Chinese, or Mexican woman. I don't even remember him dating a European, but it didn't bother him, so I didn't let it bother me either. I am told that before I roomed with him he was madly in love with an American girl who dumped him, and he never recovered. If that was so, he never mentioned it, and I never asked for confirmation or denial of the rumor.

Now here I was, standing at the Detroit Metro Airport amid the gray- and tangerine-colored vinyl chairs, waiting for him to arrive twenty years later. I wondered how we had both changed and whether we would recognize each other. I had gained weight, but through Rich's letters I learned Barry had tried to make the Olympic bicycling team, so I thought he would still be in good physical shape. As he entered the concourse from the plane's canopied runway, I saw my predilections were right. He was still physically fit and athletic looking, and the only tell-tale signs of aging were the flecks of gray hair peppering his temples. I knew he recognized me when he smiled broadly and his eyes turned to slits. Cocking his head slightly to the left as he walked toward me with his hand outstretched, he stopped suddenly and whispered while shaking my hand, "Roomie, is there a Korean guy behind me?"

"Korean?" I answered. "Well, there is an Oriental man standing back by the gate, yes."

"But is he Korean?" he persisted.

"I don't know, Barry, I can't tell. Orientals all look . . ."

"Koreans look distinctly different. Look at him closely. Do his eyes slant sideways, up, or down?"

I strained to see the Oriental, but couldn't make out his features that clearly. "Barry," I said, "I can't tell for sure. He has black hair and is slightly built."

"Roomie, you just described the entire Asian continent. Look closely . . . it's important!"

"Why is it so important?" I asked defensively. Then without waiting for an answer I shot at him, "I can't tell from here . . . he's too far away."

"Maybe we should get closer," he said as he dragged me by the lapels. He was walking with his back to the Oriental, and I was scuffling along in little choppy steps. We looked like two people who had been thrown out of a ballroom dancing class for incompetence.

"Barry, this is crazy," I said, trying not to panic.

"Why? We're getting closer, aren't we?"

"Barry, it doesn't matter if we get close enough to floss his teeth. I still won't know if he's a Korean, a Chinese, or a Pekinese."

"You'll be able to tell. Pekinese have little curly tails. This is really important, roomie! It may be a matter of life and death!"

"What does that mean?" I was beginning to panic.

"It means I've been dating a Korean woman, and I didn't know she was married. Her husband vowed revenge on me, and I think I drank some tea on the plane that may have been drugged."

"Barry, Barry . . ." I began to plead. But I didn't finish my sentence because he grabbed his throat, choked, and fell straight to the floor at my feet.

TWO

"Help him! Help him!" I heard somebody shouting from the other side of the terminal. The voice sounded familiar, but I was in such a state of panic I couldn't recall where I had heard it before.

Barry lay slumped at my feet. The left side of his face was on the floor, and his right arm covered the other side so only his hair and right ear were visible. His legs were contracted in a fetal position. To a casual observer it could have looked as if he had decided to take a nap in the middle of the Metro Airport terminal. I fell to my knees beside him to give whatever assistance I could.

"Help him! Help him!" I heard again, only louder. I still couldn't recognize the voice and looked up to see who was shouting. Passengers were walking by, hugging relatives and pretending Barry wasn't on the floor. I was able to see pant legs, shoes, ankles, and suitcases, but couldn't determine who was yelling out orders to give Barry assistance.

One young couple stopped to gawk. She was licking an ice cream cone and holding the hand of her boyfriend, who was dressed in blue jeans and a long-sleeved T-shirt with THE PERSON WHO DIES WITH THE MOST TOYS WINS printed on the chest in bright red letters. As if to prove how macho and unflappable he could be in a crisis, Mr. MOST TOYS shrugged his shoulders and said, "He's dead," tugged at his girlfriend's hand, and walked away. A Hare Krishna solicitor walked up to me, gave me a tract, then laid one on Barry's ribs. Most people seemed to think Barry was drunk and walked around him as if he were a bag of garbage placed in their path.

"Help him! Help him!" I heard a third time from right behind me. I now knew it was Lyle, the person in our quartet who was making all the arrangements for the get-together before Rich's wedding. I had not seen him since we had graduated, and except for a receding hairline he didn't look much different to me.

"Lyle," I said with a little relief, "Barry's collapsed."

"I know. I was over there and saw him get off the plane. You've got to help him."

"I'm trying, Lyle. What do you want me to do?"

He wrinkled his longer forehead quizzically and said, "I don't know. You're a preacher—what do you usually do at times like these?"

"I generally call a doctor," I answered as Lyle knelt down across from me.

"That's it? Call a doctor? Anybody can do that."

"I'm not a preacher any longer," I said.

"'Call a doctor' is all you can come up with?"

"What were you expecting, Lyle?"

"I thought you might lay your hands on him and shout, 'Heal! Heal!' or say some kind of strange prayer. What happened anyway?" he asked as he pressed his fingers along Barry's jugular vein.

"He said something about being drugged by a Korean husband on the airplane. Lyle, we'd better call a doctor."

Lyle stood up and shouted across the terminal, "Is there a doctor in the house?" He knelt by Barry again trying to find a pulse. People continued to walk by—staring, ignoring, or pretending not to notice.

"Lyle, why don't you stay here with him. I'll try to find a policeman."

"I thought we were looking for a doctor," he replied.

"We are. The police might be able to find one, plus they've got to apprehend that Korean."

"Which Korean?" asked Lyle.

"That one over there." I pointed to the Oriental man near the plane's ramp. However, three other Orientals had joined the original one. They were holding an animated conversation with heads bowing up and down.

"There's four of them," Lyle said, repeating the obvious. "Which one are you talking about?"

"The thin one with the dark hair," I answered.

"That's helpful," he said sarcastically. "You just described the continent of Asia. What's he wearing?"

"I don't remember. He's the one on the right—no, the left, I think. I don't know for sure, Lyle, this all happened so fast."

Lyle stood up again and shouted, "Is there a doctor in the house?" Kneeling next to Barry he looked at me solemnly and said, "I can't get a pulse. I think he's dead."

"We've got to stop the Korean for sure, Lyle."

"How do we round up four of them?" he asked.

"We've got to confront them."

"Are you kidding?" he shot back. "Those guys know karate. They'll kick us senseless. Rich won't have anyone who'll sit on his side of the church if we don't show up at the wedding."

"It's going to be a civil ceremony, Lyle. Besides, how do you know they can do karate?"

"They're Korean, aren't they? Those guys learn it as soon as their parents take the training wheels off their chopsticks. We don't want to fool with those guys."

"Lyle, we've got to get some help for Barry *and* stop them from leaving."

"This is awful," he said, shaking his head.

"I know."

"I made all the arrangements. A car, the condo, a big dinner, and what happens? Barry walks off a plane and drops dead. Bummer."

"I'm sure he'd apologize if he was alive, Lyle. Meanwhile we've got to act."

"Well, you're the preacher!" he said again. This time he was angry. "You deal with these kind of crises everyday. Come up with something!"

I wanted to repeat just as angrily that I was no longer a pastor, and furthermore all the time I was, I had never handled a situation where a roommate exited a plane and died from tea drugged by a jealous Korean. The panic I saw in Lyle's eyes kept me from being angry at him, however. Instead I gently said, "Lyle, stay with Barry. I'll find some help."

"All right, but hurry!" he said. I could see his hands were shaking.

I stood up, unsure of what to do first. "Is there a doctor in the house?" I shouted.

The four Koreans began to walk toward me. I prepared myself for a fight as I tried to recognize the one Barry had indicated as the jealous husband.

"Ron, Ron!" Lyle shouted.

"I know, Lyle," I replied. "I'm trying to think of something."

"Barry's awake, Ron, look! He rolled over on his back, and he's awake."

I looked down at Barry, who flashed a huge grin, eyes dancing back and forth from Lyle to me. "Boy, did I get you guys," he laughed.

"I said, 'God, help us,' and he came back to life, Ron," Lyle mumbled, as if in a daze. "You're a preacher. Why didn't you think of that?"

Barry was sitting up as the four Koreans approached us. *At least there were our three to their four*, I thought as they drew closer. The angry-husband Korean stared at Barry, who was seated in a cross-legged Indian position.

"I'm a doctor," said the Korean. "I thought I heard you call for one. May I be of assistance?"

"Our friend was dead, but now he seems better," Lyle blurted.

"Yes, he does," said the doctor as Barry stood to his feet and dusted himself off.

"I'm fine," said Barry. The other three Orientals looked at him and bowed slightly as he turned toward them. "Thank you, doctor, for your concern," Barry said, bowing at the waist as he shook the Korean's hand.

"Too much excitement perhaps," said the doctor. "A little tea and some rest might be in order."

"I said, 'God, help us,' and he came back to life," Lyle said aloud to himself as much as to anyone.

The doctor looked at him and said, "Prayer is many times the best medicine." He shook Lyle's hand, then mine, then Barry's, and the four of them walked away.

Lyle and I looked at each other stupefied.

"One lousy prayer?" mumbled Lyle.

"A Korean doctor?" I said softly.

Barry stood there laughing at both of us. "He was Japanese," he said, "but that's all right, we all look the same to them too."

THREE

His formal name was Lyle Fortrain, but he was known to us as "lyin' Lyle." Barry had seen Lyle waiting at a gate across the aisle and decided to improvise the "dying" scene as a practical joke to repay Lyle for some of the lies, practical jokes, and stories he had used to trick us over the years. In this case I was also a victim of Barry's little skit. Barry apologized to me a number of times for what he had done, although the apology was always accompanied by a smile about the successful sting he had placed on Lyle.

We didn't call him "lyin' Lyle" to his face for a long time, but he knew that was how he was labeled long before his nickname was made public. He, in fact, unofficially authorized the use of the name when we questioned a story he was telling by asking us, "Would lyin' Lyle lie to you boys?" He did it in a southern drawl, conjuring up images of a county sheriff or a used car salesman, winking one eye as he spoke. After that we called him "lyin' Lyle" or just Lyle with equal facility. But somehow when we said "Lyle," it felt as if we had left something out of his name.

Lyle had the ability to mix enough truth with his lies so it wasn't possible to tell when he was lying. Whenever I dealt with him, I thought he was telling the truth. The few times I confronted him openly, he was able to prove everything he said was fact. This tended to enhance his reputation as a great liar, and mine as being gullible and naive.

One Saturday we were golfing, and Lyle had a bet going with

one of the others in our foursome. I was the scorekeeper for the day. As we walked off the fourth green, I asked everyone their scores. "Seven," said the first. "Eight," growled the second. "Five!" chimed Lyle.

"Five!" fired Lyle's betting opponent. "I watched you over in the rough. You had a ten or eleven on this hole at least."

"I'll take it," said Lyle without batting an eyelash, and walked off to the next tee.

That's how he was some of the time. If caught in a lie which didn't seem consequential, he would own up to the falsehood and move along just as unconcerned as somebody pulling away from the drive-in window of a fast-food restaurant. He was most dangerous when he would make up a story he would tell so often and so well that he began to fool himself and accept it as the truth. He was absolutely convinced he was a kickoff return specialist on his high school football team. He told us over and over about the six touchdowns he had scored in one season, breaking the high school and conference records. Yet, when one of the doubters in our crowd called the high school for confirmation of Lyle's feat, no one remembered him being on the team let alone setting athletic records. Lyle still persisted with the story, blaming the high school for withholding information because the chairman of the board of education's son held the old record and they didn't want to upset the old man because of school politics. I actually got to the point where I believed him, but later ran into someone who attended Lyle's high school. He told me Lyle was the trainer on the football squad, and the closest he got to an end zone was when they let him chalk the lines before a game.

As we walked to the escalator that would transport us to our baggage, Barry smiled his broad grin with the slits for eyes as he teased us both. "You guys were sure a lot of help," he chuckled. "If the Detroit emergency rescue squad is looking for help, I'm going to send them your names."

"I knew you were joking all along," Lyle told him. "I was just going along with you to put the monkey on Ron's back. How did you like that little number I did about praying, Ron? Good, huh? Right in your league."

I thought it best to humor Lyle and simply nodded as we scooped Barry's bags and mine from the rubber snake transporting luggage into the terminal. Traveling by air was a rare treat for me, and I found it all too thrilling to argue with Lyle since he had paid for my airfare. The terminal was bustling with people, all of whom seemed to know where they were going, while I was awestruck by the numbers of people, cars, and commercial traffic surrounding the terminal. In addition, the thundering roar from departing jets shook the terminal building. I marveled at the sight of such huge machines getting airborne, their silver bodies groaning as they became smaller and smaller slivers in the sky.

"How are we going to get out of here?" I asked Lyle.

"I've got a limousine waiting," he said.

Barry looked at me and winked, as if to say old Lyle was at it again.

"Right. And if we don't get it back by midnight it turns into a pumpkin pulled by little mice. I've read that one. How are we getting out of here really?" Barry taunted.

"Just keep walking," he said.

"Lyle, I believed you when you told me you held the high school record for kickoff returns, but these bags are getting heavy."

We walked down a curved, gently sloping sidewalk alongside the one-way street carrying traffic to and from the air terminal. Ahead of us was a long, shiny, gleaming, white Cadillac stretch limousine. It had a V-shaped antenna on the trunk and shaded windows all around so passengers could look out but no one could see in.

"That's it, I suppose?" I fired at Lyle.

"Right," he said nonchalantly as we got within fifty feet of it. "Wait here while I deactivate the burglar alarm."

I laughed and said, "Lyle, you're good. You haven't lost the old touch. Now call us a cab or take us to your car. These bags are getting heavy."

Instead he turned a key in the door and spun another one in a small hole in the front fender of the limo. He opened up the trunk and rear doors saying, "Gentlemen, your carriage awaits."

Barry and I looked at each other dumbfounded, put our bags in the trunk, and bent into the rear seats of the limousine. As I ducked my head, Lyle whispered in my ear, "I *did* set the conference record. Look it up sometime if you don't believe me."

FOUR

L yle roared the limo away from the curb, and we entered a network of traffic. All of it seemed to be hurtling toward the same three lanes. A small, red Toyota with a bumper sticker reading, SCHOOL'S OPEN, DRIVE CAREFULLY pulled in front of us. Lyle hit the brakes to keep from smashing the little car's rear fender.

"Nice move, dog-face!" shouted Lyle to the other driver, who reached down to turn up his radio. Looking at us in the rearview mirror Lyle asked, "Have you ever noticed people who drive foreign cars act like they learned to drive in a foreign country?" As he looked at us for a response, the limo drifted into the right-hand lane. A Ford Thunderbird driver who was trying to pass us jammed his brakes and flashed a hand signal suggesting Lyle's driving was not number one with him.

"Are you sure you can drive this beast?" Barry asked.

"Sure, I can. What's that jerk trying to pass me on the right for anyhow? There's a law against that in Michigan. You guys just settle back and play with the toys."

The "toys," as Lyle referred to them, included a television, VCR, stereo, well-equipped bar, footrests, and even a seat and back vibrator. They seemed a little silly to me, but that didn't keep me from playing with them all the same. Likewise, Barry was playing with gadgets on his side of the car. We traded controls like two kids on Christmas morning, showing each other the presents Santa had brought us.

"Look at this!" I said as I zapped the television with a remote control, flipping it through five different channels.

"Check this out too," he answered by cueing a stereo disk with the push of a button. "Lyle," he yelled to the front seat, "I didn't think Hertz was in the rent-a-limo business."

"It's not rented," Lyle answered as he turned around with a big smile. As he did so, he cut off another driver who was less animated than the first, though I could read his lips and knew he was no happier.

"Can you talk looking forward?" asked Barry.

"It's a zone car," Lyle said with great pride.

"Twilight or Post Office?" Barry answered with a chuckle.

"Detroit," Lyle responded. He said it in a tone suggesting he wanted to add, "you jerk," but left it off.

"That was going to be my next guess," Barry replied. "Twilight zone, Post Office zone, or Detroit zone in that order."

I was very confused and said so.

"There are no Post Office zones anymore," Lyle smirked. "You're showing your age. How old are you now, Barry?"

"I'm confused," I said. "What's a Detroit zone?"

"The Pistons play it in basketball, but it's illegal," Barry said to me in a loud whisper. "I'm the same age as you, Lyle, forty-three."

"The Pistons don't play a zone. It's all man to man. Anyway, I'm still forty-two."

"What's a Detroit zone?" I whined as I flipped the TV channel to a game show hosted by a guy who looked like he had four thousand teeth.

"The sales zone," Lyle said again proudly. "This is the limo we use to pick up visiting dignitaries or to chauffeur board members around when they come to town." He was grinning so broadly I knew he had just told us something very important to him.

"Not just an ordinary car, but a zone car," Barry said with a touch of sarcasm.

"Ron, you're sitting in the same seat occupied by the chairman of DuPont and by the Reverend Leon Sullivan. Barry, you are resting against the same cushions that once held the butt of Henry Kissinger."

Barry tried a Henry Kissinger imitation, which he did quite well. "Not chust an ordinary car, but a zone car. Ve are riding mit da ghosts of da rich and fumous. I tink I chust made up a new vord, but den I am da smartest man in da vorld, so I can do dat."

I could see Lyle did not think Barry was funny, so I didn't laugh. "I'm impressed," I told Lyle. It wasn't a lie, but it wasn't the whole truth either. I was pleased with the effort Lyle had gone to, but I would have been just as happy in the backseat of my Chevrolet. It had never held the rear end of anyone famous though, unless you count an advance man for a Billy Graham crusade in that category.

"I figured what the heck, we haven't seen each other in a lot of years, Rich is finally biting the dust, why not bring out the big guns? It may be another twenty years before all four of us get together again."

Like a stage magician flicking his hand to produce puffs of smoke, Barry added, "Leon Sullivan, poof! The chairman of DuPont, poof! Henry Kissinger, poof! And for our finale, a zone car. Poof, poof, poof!"

Lyle shifted his eyes into the mirror with a look that told me he wasn't amused by Barry's magic act. He looked straight ahead, adjusted the air conditioner, set the cruise control, and drummed his fingers on the steering wheel.

"Where is Rich?" I asked, trying to change the subject.

"I'll tell you when we stop for dinner," he said.

"At the Zone Restaurant?" asked Barry. I shook my head at him to indicate he had said too much. Lyle didn't say a word, didn't look in the mirror, just elevated the glass between the driver's seat and us as we sped west on I-96 past a sign saying we had just entered Spartan country.

We shot past towns with wonderful sounding names— Okemos, Wacousta, Grand Ledge, Westphalia, Eagle, and Lake Odessa. I pictured the American Indians and German immigrants who must have lived in this area standing along the roadside, mystified by the sight of a huge white Cadillac blasting through their countryside while two passengers in the backseat played with televisions, VCRs, stereos, and fanny vibrators. Would they think this is progress? I wondered. I pulled at Barry's arm, signaling him to take off his headphones so we could talk. As he peeled them away from his ears, Lyle swung the big limo onto a highway exit ramp leading to the parking lot of a restaurant.

A long, cranberry-colored canopy covered its entry. Two valet parking attendants stood beneath the canopy looking like a pair of bulls whose territory had just been invaded. To them the limousine was just another car. Seeing the Lincolns, Mercedes, BMWs, and Buicks in the lot, I began to understand how they had learned to become so jaded. Instead of pulling beneath the canopy to let the bulls do their work, Lyle stopped within a hundred feet of them and kept the motor running. The dark glass separating the driver from the passenger compartment was still raised, and neither Barry nor I could see what he was doing. The bulls beneath the canopy had their heads lowered and were beginning to snort.

Slowly the dark glass was lowered, and Lyle looked at us with wide eyes and a smile suggesting another surprise for us. "Wanna talk to Rich?" he asked.

"Sure," I said quickly. "Is he here?"

"No. He's in Chicago," Lyle answered. "But then again, he's here too."

I looked to Barry for an explanation, but he just flipped his palms in the air and shrugged his shoulders to indicate he didn't understand it either.

"Open the armrest between you," Lyle said as he pointed to the console separating Barry and me. The lid of the console lifted up, and two telephones, one red and the other black, began to rise as if being levitated by a magician.

"How are you doing that?" I laughingly asked Lyle.

"Well, pick up the phone, dummies. Rich is on the line, and this is long-distance."

I giggled like a little kid. "Which one do you want?" I asked Barry.

"I'm not going to touch the red one," he whispered. "It's probably a hot line to the President."

As I picked up the red phone anyway, Lyle smiled broadly. "That one's a hot line to the President," he said.

"Of the United States?" I asked in amazement.

"Of General Motors," Lyle said, grimacing with disgust. "Who would want to talk to the President of the United States about anything?"

FIVE

Rich had been our spiritual adviser, although not in a religious sense. He had been the one person who held true to our fraternity pledge to remain "brothers throughout all time and distance, devoted to the welfare of each other and our chapter. Brothers for life." We chanted this pledge at the beginning of every fraternity meeting, and I believe we all meant it then. But time and distance proved three of us wrong. Rich was the one who never wavered in his dedication to living out the pledge regardless of the distance that separated us or the time which seemed to erode our bonds with even more devastation than the geography that kept us apart. He called each of us once a month, sent birthday cards with exact punctuality, published a quarterly newsletter about what was taking place with the four of us (as well as other members of the fraternity who were in our pledge class), and arranged the only reunion we ever had five years after graduation. Now, through his marriage, he was bringing us back together again.

We talked through dinner about Rich—his dedication to us and the fraternity. I looked back at the zeal we had put into our early years and wondered why it seemed to fade so easily for the three of us while Rich maintained a vigor that was both puzzling and admirable. I once met a man held captive in the prison camp made famous by the film *The Great Escape*. He said the survivors of the camp stayed in touch with each other every week. It was impossible for one of the survivors to become depressed without receiving six or seven caring phone calls within a two-day time span. Even Rich couldn't duplicate that kind of performance.

But it was more than Rich—it was us. I had worked with congregations who cared for each other, loved each other through all of life's hardships, and modeled Christ's principles without admonitions, sermons, or guilt trips from me. Unfortunately, I'd seen the opposite in some of my flocks also. Madalyn Murray O'Hair has been quoted as saying, "The Christian army is the only one who shoots their wounded." In my experience she may not have been entirely accurate. She left off the part about torturing the wounded before they were shot.

Rich said he would meet us in Traverse City that evening. He was driving from San Francisco to Michigan because he no longer flew anywhere. We thought this was a howl because Rich was the only one of our four who had been in the military—the Air Force, no less. Following the marriage in Michigan, Rich and his bride would continue on a honeymoon to Niagara Falls, then drive across Canada on a return route to California. Rich's construction business had been placed in the hands of a capable assistant, and, as usual, he had made arrangements for almost everything through his calls and letters.

Rich's requests had been small. He wanted Lyle to be his best man, Barry to be the usher, and I was to perform the wedding ceremony. It had nearly broken my heart to tell Rich I had been relieved of my pastoral duties and could not marry him in my church as he requested. How does one tell a friend that a congregation no longer wants you to shepherd them, that you have become a victim of a political struggle within a church which refuses to be guided by the Holy Spirit? How does one say a board of directors has voted 11 to 7 to inform you that your services are no longer needed as counselor, guide, and mentor to their spiritual growth? For months I couldn't find any way to tell him, so I chose not to. Finally, when I couldn't put it off any longer, I told him and asked him to forgive me for not being truthful from the very beginning.

His answer revealed how little I knew about his life, how preoccupied I had become with my own circumstances. "It's not that big a deal, Ron. The other guys know, but you don't—I've been living with my wife-to-be for the past two years. This was just a ceremony to make it official. I didn't want to tell you in case you couldn't marry us because of the arrangement we have. Lyle wants us to come to Michigan anyway, so we'll just have a civil ceremony."

Now the three of us exchanged stories about Rich over the baked Alaska Lyle ordered despite our protests. Halfway through, Lyle stopped himself as he was telling us a story about the time Rich and he had climbed up a five-story office building to break into a professor's office to steal a test. "Look . . . there!" he pointed at the front door.

"Very nice door," Barry said to him flatly.

"Not the door . . . The guy who just went out of it. Did you see the car he was driving?"

Barry and I shook our heads no.

"We've got to go," Lyle said bluntly.

"What about the check?" I asked.

"They'll send it to me. They know me."

"I'm just beginning to like it here," Barry said with a tease in his voice.

"Let's go . . . NOW!" Lyle barked at him.

We followed him out the door in double time. A confused hostess and waiter watched us run from the restaurant.

"Where did the guy who just left here go?" Lyle asked one of the parking attendants.

"What kind of a car do you have, sir?" the parking attendant asked, ignoring Lyle's question.

"Where did he go? Which direction?" Lyle repeated. It was clear that Lyle was agitated and that the attendant was not listening to him.

"Do you have your ticket, sir?" asked the attendant.

"You idiot!" Lyle said to the attendant as he handed him the parking stub and a ten-dollar bill.

"North on I-96," said the attendant with a smile. "Now, what kind of car is it you're driving, sir?"

"It's a zone car," Barry said sarcastically.

Lyle shot a look at Barry, then said, "You know, Gieselmann, I think you just missed another golden opportunity to keep your big mouth shut."

We jumped into the limousine as soon as it was brought to us. Lyle floored the accelerator, and we sped up I-96 as fast as he could make the limo move.

"What did I say?" Barry asked me. "Did I say something wrong? Isn't this a zone car?"

As he finished the question, the dark glass separating the driver from the passenger's compartment rose up again. I saw the speedometer needle hit 80 miles per hour just before the glass closed us in with our confusion and electronic toys.

Ten minutes after we left the restaurant, Lyle pulled the Cadillac alongside a silver Mercedes. We were going wheel to wheel. If the Mercedes went faster, Lyle sped up to stay even; if the Mercedes slowed down, Lyle did a similar move. The speed we were traveling was frightening. I was unable to ask Lyle what on earth he was doing since the glass partition was still raised. My hands began to shake as I looked out the window to see what was so special about the Mercedes. I could see the driver through the windshield, but all the other windows were darkened as in our limousine's, and thus I was unable to see how many passengers, if any, were in the Mercedes. We played this strange cat and mouse game for a distance of five miles. Incredibly, Barry had fallen asleep and was immune to the entire episode. I frantically shook him awake when I thought I saw the other driver lift a revolver with the barrel pointed upward in the ready position.

Barry rubbed his eyes almost casually as the Mercedes pulled next to us. He chuckled as he told me the driver was talking on a car phone. Barry slumped back into his seat, saying I shouldn't worry since our limousine was probably bullet-proof anyway. Within five seconds he was back asleep.

The driver of the Mercedes slowed down once again. This time Lyle did not follow his lead, but merely sped onward as if nothing had happened. A flash from the headlights of the Mercedes hit our rear windshield. I took it to mean the driver was irritated with Lyle, but within minutes we were out of each other's sight. I slumped into the thick cushions of the seat that once held the chairman of DuPont and the Reverend Leon Sullivan, both of whom I hoped were never as confused as I was at that moment.

Barry woke up as Lyle curled off I-96 onto another four-lane highway. The road signs announced we were only eighty-three miles from Cadillac, Michigan. Barry sleepily mumbled that the city could be renamed "Zonetown" as we went through. He tapped at the glass in front of us to tell Lyle he should call the mayor to make the change. Lyle ignored the tapping even though Barry persisted for a long time. Neither Barry nor I knew Lyle had an intercom system, allowing him to hear everything we had said to each other during the entire trip.

I asked Barry why he was so intent on making Lyle's life miserable in view of all the extra efforts he had taken to make our visit comfortable and memorable. "I'm just having fun," Barry teased with his wide grin.

"It's more than that," I protested.

He paused for a few seconds. "You're right. It's more than that. It's . . ." He paused even longer the second time. "It's a long story, roomie. I'll tell you about it sometime. But not now. I'm tired."

He lay his head back as if he were going back to sleep, but I knew he was faking. It occurred to me at the moment how little I knew about Barry even though we once lived together for nearly four years. He was brilliant, talented, and gifted in so many ways, yet there was a part of him that kept me an arm's length from ever knowing him intimately. I know there are some who would quarrel with the word "intimately," but a sexual connotation doesn't capture the kind of intimacy I'm referring to.

The intimate moments I had shared with my wife went beyond

sex alone. Times of openness, of being vulnerable without fear of rebuke, of sharing pleasures and pains knowing I would be heard had brought me as close to my wife, Diane, as any of our physical encounters. Perhaps the saddest I have ever been for a fellow clergyman was at a ministerial association meeting when a Catholic priest confided in me that moments of great joy were horribly painful for him. At the end of the day there was no one at home with whom he could celebrate his successes, no one who could magnify his triumphs through the act of listening. He knew as a marvelous day drew to a close there was only an empty room waiting for him. As a result he withdrew from projects which might succeed and instead volunteered only for those doomed to fail.

Perhaps I saw in Barry a reflection of my own life, and I pondered what was going wrong. Our marriage was no longer satisfactory to either Diane or me, but we seemed unwilling to deal with any solutions. I felt deserted by God—alone, unheard, and unloved in spite of all I had done for Him.

I wondered if what I was seeing in Barry was also true for me. Barry never accepted compliments, but deflected them. Nothing he did was ever good enough—it was only acceptable. What took place within him had to be a raging river, yet I lacked the courage to draw too close for fear of being swept along without being in control. I avoided talking about Christ for fear of being rejected just as I had been rejected by the church. For a moment I thought of talking to Barry about these notions, of confronting him and therefore confronting myself at the same time. Instead I pretended I was sleepy also, and I lay my head against the window as the miles to "Zonetown" grew fewer and fewer.

SIX

We didn't meet Rich in the evening as planned. When we checked into the small motel where we were scheduled to meet, the clerk handed Lyle a message saying Rich was too tired to drive any further. He would meet us before noon the next morning. Each of us went to our rooms paid for by Lyle, despite protests from Barry and me about paying our own way. "This weekend is on me, boys," he said. "Car sales are up, so bonuses are up. Besides, you two are just going to be tax write-offs at the end of the year."

The motel room had a worn, beige Berber carpet, a single bed with an orange and brown plaid bedspread, a painted white night-stand, and a yellow plastic wastebasket advertising a local Standard gas station. The flaking, black letters said, "In business in Suttons Bay since 1983." The plastic shower curtain was decorated with white and orange swans, some with their feathers and beaks coated by layers of caked soap film. Before I went to sleep that evening, I opened the nightstand to find a Gideons Bible, turned it to Genesis 22, and re-read the account of God's test for Abraham. I had read it so many times, I could nearly recite the entire passage from memory. From Genesis I turned to the New Testament accounts of the crucifixion. Abraham's test and the crucifixion had haunted me, not because of any disbelief on my part, but because I was never able to understand why Abraham's servants and those who were at the crucifixion were able to stand by so passively and allow everything to happen. I had placed

myself in the role of one of the servants who had to know Isaac
would be the sacrifice offered to God. How could a person stand
by while such a murder would be committed? Where was the call
to duty, to service, to obedience to the commandment not to kill?
Where was the compassion for Isaac within the hearts of the servants who did nothing more than unload the donkey carrying the
firewood? And at Golgotha, where were the followers of Christ
other than His disciples during the crucifixion? Why hadn't at
least one of them come forward to protest, knowing his eternal
life would be saved even if his life on this earth was taken away?
I placed myself at both scenes and shuddered at how shallow, how
depraved men could be when there is a choice between a call to
action and a chance to stand idle, allowing expediency to be the
only law worth following.

Such had been my own lot in life. I had taken a church from a
Sunday attendance of seventy-five to nearly seven hundred. Two
services were required, the Sunday school flourished, an addition
was built and the mortgage burned, and yet those who should
have supported me stood idly by while a powerful and insensitive
board voted not to renew my contract. I had married, baptized,
counseled, and buried members of the congregation. I had inter-
vened with the Father on their behalf. Yet I was being cast aside,
being crucified while the crowd stood back, being led up a mountain to be placed on an altar while the servants slept. I returned
the Bible to the nightstand, switched off the light, and listened to
the wind as it blew the waves of Grand Traverse Bay against the
shore in a black and starless night.

SEVEN

Get up you bums, get up!" Banging on my door, the door next to mine, and another, a man's voice shouted, "It's nearly ten o'clock. I've been on the road since four A.M., and you guys are still in the sack." I hastily got out of bed, pulled on a pair of pants, and stumbled to the door.

Rich was pounding on the doors of Barry's room as well as mine, but the room he thought was occupied by Lyle was opened by an elderly retired couple. The old man had a pale blue vinyl suitcase in his left hand. His wife stood behind him, a raincoat draped over her forearm as she peeked above the shoulder of her husband, who eyed Rich suspiciously.

"And you, you lyin' dog," Rich hollered before it registered that he was not dealing with Lyle. "Oh my . . . I'm sorry," he said when he realized what he had done. Rich apologized in a tone of voice suggesting he really was sorry for scaring the old couple. One of Rich's greatest attributes was his sincerity about everything he did. When he made mistakes, he was so apologetic it hurt just to listen to him ask for forgiveness. "Here, let me help you with this," he said to the old man.

Hearing the repentance in Rich's voice, the old man was steeled with a courage he knew would not be tested. "You're a maniac," he sneered at Rich. "Get out of my way or I'll have to get tough."

"No, please, I'm really sorry, sir," Rich protested. "Please, let me take this suitcase to the car for you."

The old man began to back up in tiny, choppy steps. His wife backed up with him. Her eyes flashed terror as Rich continued to pursue them into the room in an effort to get the suitcase. The old couple looked like they were doing an imitation of Charlie Chaplin walking backwards.

Rich kept saying, "Please, sir, I'd like to help."

The old man looked panic-stricken. Rich was wearing a black turtleneck pullover along with a black knit cap commonly worn by merchant marine sailors. He hadn't shaved in several days. He looked more like a cat burglar than someone trying to help an old man carry a suitcase.

Four more backward Charlie Chaplins into the room and the old man started to swing his right forearm while clinging desperately to the suitcase with his left hand. He made grunting noises like one of the Three Stooges. His wife screamed. This halted Rich momentarily. Instead of retreating though, Rich moved forward, again saying, "I'd like to help. Please, let me help."

I could see the folly in what was taking place, so I stepped into the room to pull Rich away. At that point I thought it was better for him to feel guilty for the rest of the day than to give the poor couple matching coronaries. As I entered the room, the old woman's screaming intensified. Within the confines of the little room it sounded like a police siren had just gone off. I was mystified by her screaming. What I didn't know was that Barry had walked in behind me wearing only a pair of purple boxer shorts. The old man was sure he was about to be robbed, and his wife had added something worse to the list.

Now I was saying, "I'm only trying to help."

Rich was saying, "I'm only trying to help."

The woman was screaming like a black-and-white cruiser in a high-speed chase, while the old man had expanded his repertoire to an imitation of Larry, Curlie, Shemp, and Mo all together.

The motel manager burst into the room behind Barry and me with a baseball bat in his hands.

"What's going on here?" he asked.

"Sir," Rich said in his most apologetic tone, "this is all my fault. I was looking for my friends and knocked on this couple's door by mistake."

"So what's he doing here?" he asked as he pointed at me.

"He's here to help," answered Rich.

"They were here to rob us!" blurted the old man, his wife nodding her head in agreement.

"Looks that way to me too," said the innkeeper.

Rich looked wounded and hurt. "Not true. We were trying to help. Why, my friend here is a pastor."

"And I suppose he was going to hold a prayer meeting," mused the innkeeper sarcastically. "What about him?" he asked, looking at Barry with suspicion. "What's he do?"

"I play the piano," answered Barry.

"There's no piano here!" screeched the old woman.

Barry lifted his eyebrows in mock surprise. "Well, in that case I'll just leave." He casually turned on his heel and walked out of the room.

"You really a preacher?" the motel manager asked me.

"I'm trained to be one," I said, trying to skirt the question.

"What church?" he inquired.

I hesitated for a couple of seconds, unsure of what to say. "At present I don't have one," I replied.

"Oh, one of them kind. Well, it makes me no never mind anyway. Preachers are the dumbest people in God's creation. Salvation is free, and they pay tuition for eight years at some fancy school to find it out." He chuckled at his little joke, then lowered the bat. He told us to leave and reassured the old couple they would be alright.

As we exited the room, Rich turned around and said, "I really am sorry. Really." I grabbed his arm and pulled him away as the motel manager lifted the bat once again. We went to my room. We were joined by a fully-clothed Barry three minutes later. The tension of the incident blended with the happiness of our reunion to make us giddy. We replayed the scene several times, exaggerating it with broad, burlesque behaviors.

Rich did an imitation of Barry by saying, "There's no piano in here? Well, in that case I'll just leave." Rich dropped his pants as he walked from the bedroom into the closet.

"Well, how about this?" Barry said in return. "Please, sir, I want to help. Really, I do. I swear it on a stack of Bibles, and my friend here has stacked a lot of Bibles so he would know if I'm telling a lie." He pulled the merchant marine cap from Rich's head and put it on his own to add visual impact.

First we laughed at the imitation, then Barry and I got the giggles because Rich was bald except for a fringe around his ears and the nape of his neck. Even Rich laughed at himself and rubbed his pate good-naturedly.

It was at this point that we assessed the toll the years had taken on us. I thought Rich had changed the most. In addition to his bald head, he had bags under his eyes. While he was not much heavier than when I had last seen him, he no longer walked with much energy, but seemed to take slow, stiff, measured steps. Rich teased me about my weight and thinning hair, but we both marveled at how Barry had changed so little. His hair was only lightly peppered with flecks of gray. He denied Rich's accusations of using hair coloring to keep a youthful look. There was no dispute about his physical shape, however. The skimpy outfit he wore to welcome Rich and the retirees revealed a chiseled, washboard stomach, with thighs that looked like bronze cannons set on their muzzles. Only his face, marked by fine lines and creases around the eyes, showed the signs of a few extra years. We teased each other and laughed some more when a loud banging at the door froze us into a sudden silence.

Rich opened the door cautiously at first, then threw it wide open and wrapped a big bear hug around Lyle. From the expression on Lyle's face you would have thought he had just been splashed with a basin of cold water. But he relaxed when Rich released him. Rich and Lyle pumped each other's hands, slapped each other on the back, and Lyle rubbed Rich's bald head with broad smiles. Rich was the one person I knew who had a way of tolerating Lyle's lies by either ignoring them or pretending they weren't so important. As a result, I think Lyle was more truthful with Rich than with anyone else in the world. This strange combination produced an alliance between them currently referred to (in the vernacular) as "good chemistry." As with Barry and me, Rich and Lyle had spent many hours together in their college years sharing goals, ambitions, likes and dislikes to the point of knowing each other more deeply than family members. To me it seemed the more abusive Lyle was to Rich, the more forgiving Rich became toward Lyle. Rich simply dismissed Lyle's abrupt manners and outright lies with a "that's just the way he is" statement, suggesting Lyle's behavior obviously bothered others more than it bothered Rich.

As crudely treated as Rich was by Lyle, an outsider wouldn't dare make a negative comment about Rich in Lyle's presence. At a fraternity party, two members who had been drinking made jokes about Rich's sincerity and his tolerance of Lyle's lies. The tone of their remarks suggested Rich was a coward who was afraid to face reality for fear of not being regarded as a nice guy. They didn't know Lyle was standing behind them as they acted out their farce of Rich's behavior. Lyle called out their names, asking to be invited into their discussion. When they told him to get lost he said, "You guys think you're hot stuff, huh?" He ripped a foam fire extinguisher from the wall and emptied the contents on them. As each fell to the floor, Lyle kicked one, then the other, as he poured beer on their heads. "Don't you ever talk about Rich that way again," he said as he beat them with his fists. I don't know what the final outcome might have been if three of us hadn't jumped on Lyle to restrain him. As we pulled him away from the bruised and foamy pair, Lyle was raging, arms and legs flailing, neck veins swollen like tubular balloons near the point of breaking, eyes wide-open like a cat on a hunt, with an energy level that was difficult for all three of us to keep contained.

After Rich and Lyle stopped teasing each other about changed appearances, Lyle asked what had been taking place that morning. We recounted the whole story for him, right down to Barry's purple boxer shorts and the horrified looks on the old couple's faces. Lyle's expression changed, bringing back memories of how angry he could become. "The motel manager threatened you?" he asked.

"It wasn't a threat, Lyle," Rich answered. "He was just suspicious of what was going on. You do have to admit it looked a little strange."

Lyle was fuming, "He had no right to do that. Didn't you tell him you were friends of mine?"

"No, we thought we'd try to keep him in a good mood," Barry replied.

"I'll shut this place down," Lyle growled.

Rich pleaded, "Lyle, it was a misunderstanding, that's all."

"Let it go, Lyle," I encouraged. "It's been worth a few laughs."

"I bring a lot of people up here. He has no right to treat you like that. Rich, it's your party. Tell me what you want. I'll rip his head off if you just say the word."

Rich answered very sincerely, "I want us to forget the whole thing, Lyle. Thank you for your concern. Let's get on with this get-together. I want to hear what each of you has been up to."

Lyle paused for a moment, then, as if nothing had taken place, said in a jovial tone, "All right, you jokers, let's head over to my place. It's only about five miles from here, but let me warn you, it is the most awesome place you will ever see. It's three stories tall, with walls of glass looking out onto the bay, a hot tub, sauna, private beach, the whole works. It's been designed by an architect for just this kind of occasion."

"In other words, we're staying at the Holiday Inn tonight," said Barry.

"Get in the limo, Gieselmann. You didn't think *it* existed either," Lyle shot back.

EIGHT

The house was typical Lyle, a work of deception leading you to believe one way, only to find that the reality of the situation was quite different. As we pulled the limousine onto a long, black-topped, semicircle drive, my first impression was that Lyle had once again exaggerated the size and beauty of his "summer home" in an effort to impress us. At first glance the home was a modest ranch with a rough-sawn cedar exterior. Sitting high on a bluff overlooking Suttons Bay, it was clear the view might be an attractive feature of the home, and at least we would not be staying in the Holiday Inn as Barry thought. Shafts of light broke through the tall pines, cedars, and birches edging the drive, and I felt like we were entering an enchanted forest.

As we got out of the limousine, I could feel a soft breeze from the bay accompanied by gentle washing sounds of tender waves on the shore below. Rich pulled in behind us in a Toyota pickup truck, a sore point with Lyle.

"Rich, you'll have to hide that piece of junk in the garage. I don't want my neighbors to think I'm driving a Japanese piece of crud," Lyle said seriously.

"I like it," said Barry. "It's cute."

"'Cute' is a word only women use, Gieselmann," Lyle snorted. "What kind of car do you drive? Let me guess. A European yuppie car."

"I don't have a car," Barry said flatly.

"What do you mean? Everybody has a car. Every family has 2.5 cars as a matter of fact." Lyle was looking very serious.

"I guess my job is to hold down the average then. I had a car, but I gave it to a poor Philippine couple I knew. I ride a bike everywhere I need to go."

Lyle's face flushed at the casual manner Barry used to disregard him. "I suppose those foreign women you date don't mind being taken to the movies on a bicycle," said Lyle in an effort to provoke Barry further.

"They hate it," Barry answered as Lyle grinned with triumph. "They think movies are a sign of Western decadence."

"Are you going to show us this place, or do we have to guess what it looks like inside?" I asked Lyle as he stared at Barry contemptuously.

Lyle's mood improved as he walked us past the front of the house. He described the construction and work that went into building the place. His voice took on the tone of a proud father whose daughter had just won a scholarship in addition to being named homecoming queen. Later I found Rich and Barry were no more impressed with the front of the house than I. All the while Lyle told us in detail about the "R" factor of cedar siding and "Low E" windows, plus a number of other building terms that meant a lot more to him than to the three of us. However, my view changed dramatically as soon as we entered the front door.

The foyer was white marble. A skylight in the cathedral ceiling allowed light to pass through a huge crystal chandelier, converting the sun streams into dancing darts of red, white, green and orange streaks. Beyond the foyer was a balcony with a catwalk to the right and left. Standing on the balcony, we were able to look down into a massive great room featuring a two-story fireplace on one wall. To our right was a huge master bedroom complete with a two-person whirlpool, private deck, and greenhouse. And directly in front of us was one of the most breathtaking scenes I have ever witnessed in my life. The bay stood before us as a focal point from every room in the house. The great room had two tiers of windows stacked on each other, so every inch of available wall space provided a view of beautifully clear, blue-green water, like the kind I had seen on posters of the Caribbean. The master bedroom, kitchen, lower-level bedrooms, baths, and even the basement were covered with tall, wide windows so the bay could blast its beauty at us from every direction. The bay was like a beautiful Siren right out of mythology. I was unable to keep my eyes off it. It was hypnotic in its color, beauty, silence, and suggestive lure. The three of us stood on the balcony stunned by the world we had entered as Lyle cocked his head with a smirk that suggested, "Gotcha!"

"Lyle, this is fantastic!" Rich said.

"Not the Holiday Inn, but it'll have to do," Barry agreed approvingly.

"How gorgeous the Garden of Eden must have been to be more beautiful than this," I said aloud to myself.

"Not bad for a country boy, is it?" laughed Lyle. He had come from the hills of Pennsylvania, where his father hauled coal until his lungs could haul him no further. Lyle had promised himself he would only have the best in life, and when he was hired by the Cadillac Motor Car Company, Rich wrote telling us Lyle was on his way to having all his promises fulfilled.

The next two days we reminisced, ate, lounged in the sun, and went sightseeing throughout Leelanau County. *Leelanau*, I learned, is a native American name for "land of delight." It was a most appropriate description of the time we spent together as Lyle wheeled the big, white Cadillac through small towns and cherry orchards dotting the hilly peninsula washed by Grand Traverse Bay on the east and Lake Michigan on the west.

What we weren't able to see by car, Lyle managed to show us by boat. The dock on the beach in front of his house actually berthed two boats. The first was a sailboat big enough for the four of us to live on—except for the tension developing between Barry and Lyle. The second was a powerboat we used for water skiing and running to restaurants in the area. To no one's surprise, Barry had conquered water skiing by the second day, including being able to slalom back and forth across the wake caused by the boat.

By contrast, Rich and I looked equally silly on two skis. Rich managed to get up, but would lean back too far, so when he fell he looked like a tower falling backward in slow motion. I had just the opposite problem. Once up, I would lean forward, bent at the waist with my arms straight and knees locked. When I had to negotiate a wave, I would be shot forward like a cannonball with arms and legs. The first time I went under the water I failed to let go of the rope and was dragged at least a hundred feet before Lyle mercifully cut the engine to keep me from drowning. On the second day Lyle brought a video camera to record our ineptness. It provided us with comic relief as he replayed the day's water-sport events on a wall-sized television screen.

To exaggerate Rich's slow fall backward, Lyle put the VCR on slow motion, which doubled how silly it looked. He gave me equal billing by switching the VCR to fast forward. I looked like a launched rocket until I crashed with skis, arms, and legs thrashing in the water beneath a violent spray. Watching the sun set on the second evening, I realized I had been able to forget about my personal problems. For the first time in months I had actually laughed at myself.

I thanked Lyle in the evening for the wonderful time I was having. He actually blushed. For a moment I thought he wanted to talk to me in private, but Rich walked in singing the old fraternity sweetheart song. Rich said this was the song he wanted the three of us to sing at his wedding.

NINE

The next day the rains came. During the first day we told jokes, compared stories about people we remembered (there were surprisingly few), and talked about what other professions we might have chosen. Men, it seems, are obsessed with talk about their jobs. Women, by contrast, are willing to talk about people, emotions, likes, dislikes, their bodies, children, friends, and husbands. As I see it, men can talk about their jobs and sports openly; everything else is too risky. I enjoyed my work, in part, because I was able to deal with women who seemed more complete than the men in my church. But neither men nor women brought my demise as a pastor. A committee did.

The more we talked about jobs, the harder it seemed to rain. There was no place in Leelanau County Lyle could take us that we hadn't seen before. We had eaten all the food we could hold, so more talk about professions was inescapable. Lyle's success as an Assistant Zone Manager for Cadillac was obvious by the house, its furniture, and the electronic gadgets filling his "summer home." Lyle liked to talk about his job, how he worked with struggling dealers to make them successful and helped new business ventures get off the ground.

Rich was the president of a San Francisco construction company specializing in apartment complexes and commercial buildings. The misfortune of the earthquake played into his hands as a windfall, turning disaster for others into a lucrative business for him. He had many humorous stories about subcontractors, leasing agreements, and insurance claims. I didn't think it was possible for there to be a funny story on any of those subjects, but Rich brought life and humor to each one.

Barry was a math professor at one of the premier universities in the East. At age thirty-five he took a sabbatical to determine once and for all whether or not to be a concert pianist. He bought a vacant factory which once housed forty-five women and sixty-eight sewing machines making women's summer dresses and maternity clothes. The lower level was converted into a dance studio for serious ballet students, one half of the upper level was rented to aspiring artists who needed a loft with a northern exposure, and the other half of the upper level became Barry's practice area. Four months of piano practice for six hours a day, seven days a week, plus maintaining the studios, collecting money from wayward tenants, and listening to continual complaints caused Barry to rethink his ambitions. Two months later he sold the factory and decided to try out for the Olympic bicycling team instead.

At a critical time trial in Columbus, Ohio, he was leading the pack through thirty-seven miles. (I later learned being the leader is not the strategy a serious biker normally employs.) Somewhere at that point, Barry turned the wrong way and lost all kinds of precious time. Although he ultimately placed fifth overall, it was not good enough to be considered for the team. Barry told these stories very seriously. Never did his eyes disappear into the familiar slits formed by his wide smile. It was obvious he had not told these stories to many people. He paused a number of times to make sure his account was accurate. He interjected no anecdotes to add spice to the telling of his life.

At the conclusion of Barry's bicycle story, Lyle broke out laughing as if he had just listened to the funniest joke he had ever heard. It was an evil laugh, full of mockery and arrogance. I felt sorry for Barry, but didn't know what to say. Rich tried to change the subject, but Lyle kept laughing and repeating, "He turned the wrong way. I don't believe it. There are only two ways to turn, and he went the wrong way."

It rained that entire day, that evening, and was still pouring when I got up the next morning. Rich and Lyle were drinking coffee at a table in the breakfast nook. Dark clouds drilled large drops of rain against the windows with the irregular staccato of a snare drummer gone mad. As I joined them, each grunted a greeting with little enthusiasm. We wordlessly watched the rain beat its way across the bay as if it was aiming a path directly at the walls of windows protecting us from its frenzy.

From a lower-level bathroom I heard Barry humming and singing cheerful, upbeat songs. He continued the happy medley as he came up the stairs to the trio of silent coffee-sippers at the breakfast table.

"Aren't we happy!" I said to him.

He flashed a whimsical little grin but didn't respond verbally. His humming continued as he opened kitchen cupboards in an effort to find a cup.

"Turn the right way, Gieselmann," growled Lyle. "I'd hate to see you get lost in a kitchen."

Barry winced as he put a teakettle on the stove while dropping a tea bag into the cup. His humming changed to whistling as he vainly tried to match a song to the drumming of the rain on the windows. He opened a book he had brought from upstairs while he waited for the water to boil.

"There's coffee already made," Rich said.

Barry answered, "I drink tea. Never developed a taste for coffee."

Lyle blurted, "You don't drink coffee, you wear purple underwear, you don't drive a car, you're forty-three years old, never been married and still use words like 'cute.' I'm beginning to wonder about you, Gieselmann."

I didn't say anything, hoping Lyle's crude comments would soon be followed by an apology. For a moment I thought Barry ignored the remarks completely. He moved to the table with his tea, gave a loud exhale, and fixed a hard stare at Lyle. Barry took a color photograph from the book he was reading, placed it on the table in front of him, and said, "Lyle, I think you've got a problem. This guy is having his picture taken with your wife and kids."

Barry slid the photo across the table. Although I couldn't determine all the details, I could see Lyle's summer house in the background, with a man, woman, two children, and a miniature schnauzer in the foreground. The positioning of the group suggested a family portrait with each person professionally posed.

"Where'd you get that?" asked a shocked Lyle.

"It was in this book. On the back it says, 'The Mirkin Family,' and it was taken last month."

"It is the Mirkins. They were here last month for a visit, and we had their pictures taken. That's not my wife and kids." Lyle's hands trembled slightly, and his voice became louder.

Barry answered in a patronizing way, "That was real nice of you, Lyle. Since you know the Mirkins so well, you might tell Mr. Mirkin he left several Cadillac sales plaques with his name on them in a dresser drawer in my room. He also left a photo album of this house along with a diary of its construction. He and his family must have been around here often. They are in almost every picture. You sure like to take pictures of them, don't you?"

"What were you snooping around in the dressers for?" asked a hostile Lyle.

"It's where I store my purple underwear. And my tea bags. Cute, aren't I?"

"You had no business nosing around in other people's property! I told you I let the Mirkins use this place. That was all. They used it last month. It's true. You can call them if you like."

Rich and I knew Lyle was lying again. We looked at each other, unsure of what to say.

Barry kept boring in. "There are also a number of places where pictures have been taken off the walls in this house. Maybe you should call this Mirkin guy. It looks to me like he might be robbing you blind."

"You want to call him?" Lyle asked desperately. "Here, I'll give you his number. I've got his number right here." Lyle rummaged through kitchen drawers in search of a phone book.

Barry answered, "I've got his number. He left several business cards in the dresser with his home number and his work number. Of course, you must know his work number off the top of your head because his card says he's the Assistant Zone Manager for Cadillac at the same office where you work. I guess there are two of you who are assistants, right? Or is one of you the Assistant and the other is the assistant to the Assistant? I get confused about those kinds of things."

"That's it. I'm the real Assistant Zone Manager. He just carries the title."

By now it was obvious Lyle was clutching at straws. Even though I was the most gullible of the group, I could hear the panic in his voice and see the terror in his eyes. "It's all right, Lyle. Why don't you tell us what's really going on?" I said as sympathetically as I could.

He looked away from me and stared at the sheets of rain coming in our direction.

"He's right, Lyle," Rich said as he stood up and placed his hand on Lyle's shoulder. Lyle looked up at Rich with such sorrow on his face I thought he was going to cry. "I wanted this to be a fun event for you, Rich. I wanted it to be first-class all the way."

"This isn't too shabby," Rich laughed.

"Yeah, and it isn't mine either," Lyle confessed. "Gieselmann caught me. I even got over here early just to make sure I didn't miss anything on the same day you three were at the motel playing games with the old geezers. I never thought to look in all the dresser drawers. And who would have thought to check the books for a photo? Mirkin is such a slob, though, I shouldn't be surprised."

Lyle pushed away from the table and paced around the kitchen, stopping on occasion to take a sip of coffee or a short pause to collect his thoughts. The tension had broken, and his story rolled out from him with little prompting.

TEN

"Just listen to me, all right? I don't need you to ask me a lot of questions, and I don't want you to feel sorry for me. All I want is someone to listen to what I say. Nobody has done that for the last two years, maybe more." This was how Lyle began his account. We honored his wish, not interrupting or asking questions until he had finished. Although I am naive about when I am being lied to, I believed Lyle's story to the letter. From the looks on the faces of Rich and Barry, they felt the same as I.

He moved to the lower-level great room. Lyle began with his back to us, looking at the bay and speaking to the wall of windows. At one point he turned around to face us, although we each dodged any direct eye contact. We pretended to clean our nails, tie our shoes, or look at the bay as if something captivating was taking place on it during the downpour.

"Fifteen years ago I started with Cadillac," he said. "I had knocked around on different jobs, but nothing seemed to click. I was determined to make this job the one that would pay me the most, to provide Louise and me with a standard of living I had dreamed about since the day I left the coalfields. I had a few flunky clerical jobs when a chance to move to marketing came my way. I loved it right from the start. Everybody I worked with had this attitude of not being just like any other person on earth. You were a 'Cadillac' person—the best, the classiest, the world standard. I don't think I could say three sentences to anyone without saying the word Cadillac. There were dealers and deals, cars and limos, incentives and programs, marketing and promoting. I loved it. I mean I *LOVED* it. I wasn't part of Cadillac—I was Mr. Cadillac in the flesh.

"I got transferred around to different locations. I can't even name them all. I know there was Houston, Atlanta, Chicago, and Detroit. It didn't matter where I was sent or when they wanted to send me. I just went. The kids attended six different schools in a period of eight years. We got notice of a new transfer one time as the moving van was unloading into the house we had just purchased from the last transfer. We spent four weeks in that house. That is, Louise and the kids did. I moved to the next location and waited for them.

"Somewhere along the line, probably Chicago, Louise met somebody else. I suppose she was trying to tell me, but all I really wanted to hear was my boss telling me I was on the path to being a Zone Manager."

At this point Lyle turned around to face us. "Doesn't sound that unusual so far, does it? Man gets consumed by job, loses wife and kids. Must be hundreds of stories like it every day. Here's a little something extra, though. Old Lyle doesn't do anything unless it's first-class. In this case, it's first-class crazy.

"The guy Louise ran away with is a big electrical contractor in Chicago. At least, that's his cover. He's into something else, but I don't know what. Might be gambling, prostitution, laundering money. Something rotten for sure. Louise called me early last summer to say she was worried about what business her new husband had going beyond the electrical world. Two weeks later she was dead.

"Rich, when you would call I couldn't bear to tell you what happened. I never let on we were even divorced, let alone that Louise was dead. I kept hoping you'd stop writing those newsy letters to all of us so I wouldn't have to lie about what really took place.

"At any rate, she and her husband left Chicago one night by sailboat, headed for Saugatuck, Michigan. She was supposedly drinking that night and fell overboard while her husband slept below deck. It doesn't make sense in a couple of ways. Louise hardly ever drank, never to excess. She didn't know how to navigate a boat, and for sure not at night.

"I went to the funeral, and her husband hardly looked at me. Now I see his face everywhere. He's a big roller, drives a silver Mercedes. I see a silver Mercedes and I go crazy. I was sure that was him on the highway the other night. I'd like to kill him. I know he killed Louise, and part of me died with her. The kids are messed up. Both are in college, but neither want to talk about her. Neither want to talk to me.

"Now here comes the clincher. For the past two years I've been working night and day, buttering up the Assistant Zone Manager. I've been here on weekends helping him put in the dock where his boats are berthed. I've painted the place, baby-sat for his two bratty kids, and helped him haul the boats in and out of the water every spring and fall.

"Ten months ago he gave me this junky assignment to coordinate a national golf tournament Cadillac was going to sponsor. This on top of the fact I've got the highest burnout job in any zone—a Distribution Manager. That's a clever title for a person who gets to call dealers when cars aren't selling and convince him he can handle another two or three truckloads. The dealer gets to scream at me and remind me he has to pay a floor plan—inside word for interest on these cars, and I can put them anywhere I want, but not on his lot. I have to convince him he just needs to push a little harder, and if I don't, I know *I'm* going to get pushed out the door. During good times the dealers are calling me and screaming for more cars, especially the hot-selling ones. I have to tell them the system is fair and they'll get a proper allotment. But if a dealer squawks to my boss, you can bet who hears about unfair treatment.

"So anyway, I've got this high-pressure job and now I've inherited a golf tournament too. I'm working sixteen-hour days just to stay even. I haven't had a Saturday off in the last year unless you count coming up here to work as time off. The tournament went together perfectly. It was organized right down to the color of the stripes in the scorer's tent. Mirkin, the Assistant Zone Manager, calls me in one day with a great big grin on his face. This is it, I think. I'm on my way to an Assistant's job of my own.

"'Fortrain,' he says, 'you did a heckuva job on the tournament. In addition, car sales are up for the past four quarters in a row. I've got some good news for both of us.'"

Lyle became more animated, pacing back and forth, swinging his arms, running his fingers through his hair. He looked older, more stoop-shouldered. His skin had a pallor matching the clouds and rain outside.

"Man, my heart was beating. I could hear it say, 'this is it, this is it, this is it.' Mirkin proceeds to tell me the good news for him. As a result of the organizing effort for the tournament, he and the Zone Manager and their families get to spend a week in Palm Springs at the club where the tournament will be played. I work my head off and he gets to go to the tournament.

"I think to myself, 'Is that all? Where's the good news for me?' Then Mirkin unveils the big surprise. 'Lyle,' he says (he always calls me by my first name when it's something crummy coming up), 'Lyle, I've got a new job for you. I want you to be the Operations Manager for the zone.'

"I'm stunned. I don't even know what an Operations Manager is. We don't have such a job. I think maybe they've renamed the Assistant Zone Manager's job to Operations Manager and I've got it, but I don't know whether to be happy yet or not. Instead, I play it cool and ask what an Operations Manager is. Mirkin tells me it's the distribution job along with the supervision of everyone in the zone office. They did away with the Office Manager, so I get to do both jobs. That's my new job—Operations Manager. Mirkin tells me in another five or six years I'm sure to be an Assistant Zone Manager. Huh! In another five or six years I'll be pushing fifty, and there are so many young, hard-charging kids out there now that I'll be too old for an Assistant's job. I'm done! All that work, a dead wife, two kids who hate me, and I'm an Operations Manager!

"Mirkin says he wants me to know how much he appreciates

what I've been doing, and while times are tough for the company, he wants to do something out of his own pocket. He handed me the keys to this place and told me to use it while he's away in Palm Springs. Luckily you scheduled your wedding during this time, Rich, otherwise we'd be staying in a two-bedroom apartment in Farmington. Then Mirkin lays the real killer on me. He says would I mind taking the limo up north with me and meet him and his family at the airport right after Labor Day. They'll be coming back from Palm Springs, and he wants to close up the place. In fact, if I get a chance, I might want to put the sailboat away, have it winterized, and pull up the dock since they won't get a chance to use it anymore this season.

"That, gentlemen, is the story. It is 'a tale told by an idiot, full of sound and fury, signifying nothing.' It is the truth, the whole truth. Lyin' Lyle is done lyin'. I'm through with it all. I'm quitting after the wedding, Rich. In the meantime let's have some fun." With this he turned back to the bay, and the tears rolled down his cheeks as fast as the rain ran down the windows. He cried silently at first, but his shoulders began to shake and he couldn't contain his grief any longer.

I put my arm around his shoulder. He buried his head in my chest like a little child, his back and shoulders heaving as he sobbed. We rocked back and forth as the clatter of the rain mocked Lyle's breaking heart.

What none of us knew at the time was that we still did not know the whole truth.

ELEVEN

That night we got drunk. I hate to admit it, but it's true. I hadn't had anything to drink for at least seven or eight years because I didn't think it set a good example for others in the church. But I wasn't the leader in a church anymore. A clan of the self-righteous and self-proclaimed took care of that.

It had rained the entire day, and we were unable to escape the aura of Lyle's agony. We had become a bas-relief, four people frozen by their inability to deal with the torment of life, ambition, and failed dreams of a friend. We spent the day avoiding conversation. A black, baby grand piano in the great room with the gold-leafed name of Charles Frederick Stein above the keyboard became Barry's refuge. He played all afternoon, varying from classical to show tunes. Rich wrote letters after failing to make a phone connection with his bride-to-be. I found a historical novel on Pontius Pilate. While it really didn't hold my attention, it kept me from talking to anyone else. Lyle opened his briefcase, then immersed himself in a series of reports for work with the aid of a lap-top computer and a pot of black coffee. Late in the afternoon we were all bored with our diversionary activities, but we were afraid to stop doing them because then we would have to face each other again—most especially Lyle.

Rich was the first to break the silence. "You know what I've got a craving for?" he asked cheerily. "Pizza. We haven't had a pizza since I got here. Let's get a pizza and some beer."

Barry shook his head. "I'd rather have Chinese."

Rich grimaced. "Chinese food and beer? They don't mix."

"How about some Mexican food?" I suggested.

"Mexican food and beer go together," said Rich. "I could do Mexican."

"Somehow I get the impression you're more interested in the beer than food," I said with a laugh.

"Beer, that's what we could get," Rich agreed. "I've had a real craving for beer."

"Lyle, do you know of any places around here that sell pizza, Chinese food, Mexican food, and beer?" Rich asked.

Lyle simply shook his head no.

Rich came back with, "Any places that sell just beer?"

Lyle spoke for the first time since morning. "Sure, plenty."

"Well, then it's settled." Rich smiled enthusiastically. "We'll go out to get the beer, have the other stuff delivered."

·And that is exactly what we did. The four of us piled into Lyle's white Cadillac limousine, affectionately dubbed "Zonecar," and headed off to town. We each bought two eight-packs of beer, a couple bottles of wine, some chips, pretzels, and a variety of gums and penny candies.

The other three began to drink in the car on the way home. In truth I regretted going along with the idea, but didn't have the nerve to say I was not going to join them. Lyle and Rich had already finished two cans of beer by the time we got back to the house. Barry sipped from a wine bottle. I just kept looking out the window wondering if it would ever stop raining.

Rich and Lyle had finished four cans of beer and Barry was halfway through a bottle of wine before I began drinking. There was no pressure from them. I somehow felt left out of things—for the past two months of my life I had felt left out of everything— so I started drinking along with them. Lyle's mood began to turn less somber as he felt the effects of the beer combined with no food since morning. With only one can of beer in me, plus the absence of food, plus years of abstinence, my head started to feel light. Barry wasn't talking as much as Rich, but his eyes were starting to disappear into their familiar slits as he smiled and laughed at anything being said. Within another half hour, we were all drunk. Perhaps we could have been declared legally sober, but based on the conversation we had, we were not in our right minds.

"Sssay," said Lyle a little hoarsely, "I wanna 'pologize to you guys for lyin' to you. Especially you, Richie. I wanted this be memorable, and I messeditup." He was running words together. It was difficult to follow him since my listening was also impaired.

Rich got a sorrowful, repentant, wrinkled-forehead look. "Are you kiddin' me? This is great. I'm with my bes' buddies in the worl' an' pretty soon I'm gonna get married."

Barry said, "Rich, don' wrinkle your forehead when you look sad. Now that you got no hair, it wrinkles from your eyebrows, all the way over your ears, and down the back of your collar."

"He's doing an imitation of one of those Chinese dogs. What do you call them?" I asked giddily.

"Moo goo gai pan," said Barry. "We forgot to order food."

"Noooo, tha's not the name," I said with a frown. "I know it as well as my own."

"Mu shoo pork," Barry laughed.

"Tha's not my name," I said testily.

"Cashew chicken gai ding," Barry responded.

"Tha's it!" I answered.

"Your name is cashew chicken gai ding?" Barry giggled.

"No, tha's the name of the Chinese dogs with all the wrinkles." I laughed. "Actually they just call them cashew chickens for short."

"A dog is called cashew chicken?" asked Barry incredulously. "Remind me to never order that again."

"What's gai ding then?" Lyle joined in.

"It's an ole radio show where a guy flies around with his niece and nephew," I said. They all groaned.

"That's awful," Rich howled.

"Sure is," I agreed. "I always liked the banking show better."

"What show waszat?" Lyle asked.

"The loan arranger," I said with a burst of laughter. They all threw pretzels and chips at me.

"I hate banks," Rich said seriously. "They cause' me to go belly up."

"If you had a belly like Ron's, you could have bounced right back," Barry said as he uncorked another bottle of wine.

Now I was throwing pretzels and chips at Barry.

"I'm dead serious," Rich said as seriously as one can when drunk. "Lyle, you aren' the only one who lied here. I'm not the presiden' of any construction company. I'm the head of a maintenance crew who cuts grass and cleans toilets for commercial buildings in San Francisco. I got four illegal immigrants and a '63 Chevy pickup truck to my name. The bank repossessed everythin' else I got."

"IzzzzO.K., Richie," Lyle slurred. "I know how you feel. By the way, would you like to buy a Cadillac?" They both laughed and hugged each other.

"I'm totally serious," said Rich. "I got very little to my name. Even the Toyota truck belongs to my future brother-in-law. The '63 Chevy would never make it 'cross country."

"I'll settle for a pizza," Barry said. "I'm starving."

"Well, pick up the phone and order a couple dozen, professor," said Lyle who looked happier knowing Rich was not the president of a construction company.

"I'm going to do just that. And don' call me professor. While we're on the subject of true confessions, I don' teach math at the university level either."

"Oh, oh," I said.

"I teach remedial English and basic math to minority females, most of 'em pregnant, who dropped out of high school and are trying to qualify for a high school equivalency. School I'm at was set up by some smooth-talking black guy who got a grant of ninety trillion dollars, or something like it, from the federal government. I never took a sabbatical—I just quit the job at the university. Now they have grad students teaching basic algebra and business math. I don' have a doctorate, so I'm not too useful to universities. They tol' me I'm not needed."

"Banks own the universities," said Rich. "It's all a part of the system." He gulped another beer, then burped.

"I'm beginning to agree with you," said Lyle, whose eyelids had sunk to half-mast. "If the banks didn' put high interest rates on the cars, the dealers wouldn' put pressure on the zone, and I might be Assistant Zone Manager by now."

"Banks make student loans impossible. That's why I'm where I'm at today," chimed in Barry jokingly.

"And if the banks would have given us a lower interest rate, the church would not have had to struggle to pay off the mortgage, I'd be employed today," I said just to say something.

"I hate banks," Rich grumbled.

"I'm hungry," Barry repeated. "What kind of Chinese food do you eat?"

"Shar-peis!" I shouted.

"I never had that. What is it?" Lyle asked.

"The Chinese dog," I answered.

"Let's order pizza," Rich mumbled. "Chinese like too much dog meat in their food."

PART II

TWELVE

By the time the pizza came, we had begun to sober up. We drank a large pot of coffee Lyle made after the four of us wolfed down three large pizzas. Even Barry drank coffee, which seemed to please Lyle. I was amazed once again at how the little things in life are made so important by each of us. My wife wore a pink, raw silk suit to church one Sunday, and some members of the congregation were upset because we were being too worldly, poor stewards of our money. The next week she wore an older, more conservative gray tweed, and others wondered if I was mistreating her. I failed to greet one senior citizen as she exited the church after a Sunday service. This led to a withdrawal of her membership, along with a stern letter about my "uppity ways." Putting a pot of black coffee on top of a stomach full of gooey pizza is not my idea of a health-food combination. Yet that combination made a healthy difference to Lyle in terms of his attitude toward Barry.

"Gieselmann," Lyle said with a tone of embarrassment, "I'm sorry I've been riding you lately. The cracks about the purple underwear and riding the bicycle the wrong way were out of line."

Barry seemed equally embarrassed by Lyle's apology. Maybe one of the reasons I liked women in the church is that they are nurturing when problems arise. Contrary to popular mythology, men do not confront problems, they avoid them. Men would prefer to pretend a problem doesn't exist in the hope it will solve itself or go away rather than deal with it openly. Women are willing to admit there is a problem and generally think they can love it away. Barry fit the pattern like all other men by saying, "It was no big deal. It didn't bother me."

Lyle was not going to back off, however. It had taken him so long to develop the courage to talk to Barry that a quick line or two on the subject would not be sufficient. "Did you ever wonder why I needle you so much, Gieselmann? Have you noticed I call everyone else by their first name, but I call you by your last? I did it all the time we were in college together, and I'm still doing it today. Didn't you ever get curious about that?"

"Can't say I have," Barry said without much conviction.

"Because I've been jealous of you. All these years I've been jealous of everything you've done or were capable of doing. You can play a piano well enough to think about going on a tour. I get lost in the second verse of 'Heart and Soul.' You think of entering the Olympics at age thirty-five while I'm wondering if I have enough strength to push the remote control on the TV to watch the Olympics. I've been jealous of you from the time we were in calculus together. I had to study ten hours a night plus develop a full range of cheat sheets just to pass. You would spend a half hour each day and get straight A's. Now I find out you can drink coffee just like the rest of us. You're O.K. in my book."

"Drinking coffee has brought all this on?" Barry asked with his eyebrows raised.

"Well, that and the fact that you're a flunky like all the rest of us. I mean teaching a class at Yo' Momma's High is not the same as being head of the math department at Princeton. But it is in the same league with the rest of us failures in life."

"We're not failures," I objected. "We're all God's creatures."

Lyle replied, "So are skunks and parasites, but we're only a half-step above them. Look what we've got here. We make the Marx brothers look like the Einstein quartet. Chico is a failed car peddler whose wife runs away with a hoodlum, then ends up doing an imitation of Flipper. Harpo is a piano player disguised as a math and English teacher for women who think gestation means a place where jokes are parked. Groucho is a preacher who loves everybody, but nobody loves him back. And Zeppo subscribes to the *Dirty Toilet Journal* to keep up on his professional reading. You don't think that qualifies as four failures? We are the biggest group of clowns since the circus came to town."

"I don't have to listen to this garbage," Barry said as he discarded his pizza plate, beer cans, and coffee cup.

"You can't run from it, Gieselmann," Lyle said eagerly. "You're just like the rest of us. We are gainfully employed bums. That is, except for Ron, but he'll get another church sometime. No offense, Ron."

The back of Barry's neck was starting to turn crimson. "Lyle, if Cadillac doesn't want you anymore, I'm sure the State Department needs smooth talkers like you as ambassadors to Siberia or Tibet."

Lyle was rolling and ignored Barry's comment. "Guys, we've got to face it. We count for nothing on the face of this earth. We have added nothing. We are zeroes without the rims. We've avoided success like crazy. Gieselmann, you're still single. I'll bet you've met plenty of women who would marry you, but you wouldn't take the risk. The rest of your life is a list of almosts as long as your arm. You almost went on tour, you almost made the Olympic team, you almost got your doctorate. You've got all the talent a person in this life should ever need, and the closest you get to the winner's circle is *almost* making it. You know the story of my life. I've been devoted to a career costing me the three living people I thought meant everything to me. Obviously they didn't. They needed a Cadillac crest on their foreheads to get any attention from me. Ron, you're the preacher, I know that means you can't tell a lie. Are you happily married? Do you feel fulfilled?"

I stammered, "I, uuuh, I, I uuuh, I don't know how to answer those questions. I don't think anyone who is out of a job feels fulfilled."

Lyle wouldn't let me alone. "All right, just answer the first question. It only requires a yes or no. Are you happily married?"

Instead of help from the other two, I was met with silence. I went a long time without answering. Finally I confessed, "No, I'm not. But we're working on the problem. Diane has her career and . . ."

"Everybody's got their career!" Lyle exclaimed. "What difference does that make? If you took everybody who accomplished anything, who really did something bold and daring with their lives, you'd be lucky to fill a high school stadium in the state of Rhode Island. The rest of the United States would be populated with people who have their careers. We haven't mattered one tiny bit. Even Rich, the only one of us who didn't avoid the military during the Viet Nam War, outslicked Ho Chi Minh and Uncle Sam at the same time. Tell 'em where you earned your combat pay as a Viet Nam era veteran, Richie."

Now Rich was stammering. "Lyle, uuuh, this has, uuuh . . . this is . . . that is . . . This has turned kind of ugly, hasn't it?"

"Just tell them," Lyle smirked. "I will if you don't."

"I was stationed in Denmark," Rich said sadly.

"Keeping it safe for democracy," Lyle teased.

"It was part of the NATO alliance," Rich argued sheepishly.

Barry could sit still no longer. He too paced around the room stealing glances at the reflections off the bay. Lights from houses on the other shore were reflected in the water like shards of glass from a broken window. Barry took deep breaths, nostrils flared wide, teeth clenched tight as Lyle spoke.

"So what's the solution, Fortrain?" Barry demanded. "Nothing will bring your wife back. Your kids might talk to you sometime. I'm not going on tour, I'm too old to try out for the Olympics again. Rich can't start another war just to satisfy you. And Ron's dismissal won't be reversed. What's done is done. So what?"

Lyle smiled. "I do have an answer, Gieselmann. I propose we use our remaining time together to do something really bold, a high-risk adventure nobody can take away from us. Let's create a plan and execute it so every contingency is covered. We'll be nobody's victims anymore. Our destiny will be up to us. We won't have to worry about the Mirkins, the church boards, or university policies for this one."

Rich looked confused. "I thought I was sober. Have I been drinking again? What are you talking about?"

Lyle was grinning broadly. He was animated, even charming. "You thought of the solution, Rich. It was right in front of us all the time."

"Did I black out?" Rich asked. "I did that once. I shouldn't drink anymore."

"It's up to us this time, gentlemen. We can declare our independence from the whims of others. We can taste the success of a delicious mission that will hinge solely on our own planning, wits and courage." Lyle's years of negotiating with car dealers was showing. I didn't know what he was talking about, but he sounded so convincing, his idea was automatically attractive based on the charm of his presentation.

"Does that sound appealing to you? Does that sound like something you'd like to pursue? Wouldn't you like to look back on your life with a self-satisfaction no one could ever take away from you?"

Rich, Barry, and I traded glances with each other. I was hoping to catch some body language from either of them to see if they knew what Lyle was talking about.

Rich broke the ice with, "I don't know what you're selling, pal, but I'll take two!"

"It was your idea, so you should," retorted Barry.

Rich said quizzically, "Remind me what it was again. I went to the bathroom a few times and forgot."

"Banks, Rich, banks. Remember how you said you hate banks?"

"I'm with you so far," Rich nodded.

"We're going to rob a bank," said Lyle in a matter-of-fact tone.

"Lyle . . ." I began but was interrupted.

"Just hear me out. Here in Suttons Bay there is this little bank. It has only three tellers and an old man who sits in an open office shifting pencils from one side of his desk to the other. We'll stake out the place and rob it without the use of guns or anything violent. Just a note to a teller and away we go. Or maybe we find a way to sneak in there at night, pop open the safe. We can work out the details later."

"You're nuts," said Barry.

I couldn't keep quiet. "It's beyond the law, Lyle—man's law and God's. You know I can't participate in such an act." I wanted him to reflect on the gravity of this discussion, but he countered too quickly.

"Man's law, maybe, but not God's law. Where does this need to achieve something come from? Why does the Protestant ethic work so well? God expects us each to achieve something in our lives."

"Something morally and spiritually uplifting, not illegal," I answered.

"Not at all," he said. "We are simply to *achieve*. History will determine whether or not it was uplifting. Mother Theresa's sisters and those who burned Joan of Arc at the stake both thought they were answering God's calling. One group is treated favorably, the other is not. The Crusaders killed women and children, yet today they are called followers of the Lion-Hearted. What we are to do in this life is to use our talents, to do something bold with our lives. Historians can determine whether we chose the right path or not."

"I'm going to bed," Barry said.

"Gieselmann, you can't run from it any longer. You're the most talented guy here. Here's a chance to use all those skills for one wild adventure where *almost* is not an option." Lyle had a grin on his face as he pointed his finger at Barry.

Barry took two steps up the staircase and halted.

"Look, I don't give a hoot about the money. Money's the last thing on my mind," Lyle protested. "A little jerkwater town like this probably doesn't have much in the till anyway. I'm talking about the adventure of it all . . . The idea of planning something that can only be pulled off through our teamwork and wits. As far as I'm concerned, we can dump the money in the bay or give it to our favorite charity."

"No guns? No violence?" asked Rich.

I was shocked. "Rich, you're going to be married in less than a week."

"Yeah, but I don't love her. She gave me an ultimatum to either marry her or move out. I don't make enough on my own to pay the rent for a place like we're living in now. Her income plus mine keeps us going, so I figured marriage didn't sound that bad. I'm not getting any younger. I'm not so hot-looking either."

"You sound like you're going along with this craziness," I said.

"Ron, Ron, Ron," Lyle pleaded, "I'm not asking for any commitments tonight. Heck, we've been drinking, we've had a tough day together. All I'm asking is to think about it. We could stake out the place for a couple of days, and if it seems feasible we'll do it. If not, we forget the whole thing."

"What do I have to lose?" asked Rich. "'Nothing ventured, nothing gained' is the old saying."

"Is it all right if I go to bed now?" Barry asked.

Lyle nodded his head. "Gieselmann, you get a good night's sleep. I want you to be plenty rested for our morning meeting. The meeting begins at 8. Coffee will be ready at 7."

THIRTEEN

I told myself the pizza and coffee were keeping me awake, but I knew the real reason was the tone of voice used by both Rich and Lyle. It was clear to me they were serious about robbing a bank, and I had to find some way to keep them from it. I thrashed around in my bed, freed from any hope of sleep or useful ideas.

I heard noises from the bathroom down the hall, followed ten seconds later by a light tapping on my door. It was Barry. He was wrapped in a short, white terry cloth robe and was casually drying his hair. "You're not asleep either?" he asked.

"Coffee get to you?" I asked in return.

"Same thing's keeping me awake that's keeping you awake. I don't know about you, but I'm out of here tomorrow."

"We can't do that, Barry. Rich and Lyle will try this stunt on their own. I can hear it in their voices."

"I can too. That's why I'm out of here."

"We've got to keep them from it," I insisted.

"They're big boys now, Ron. We aren't going to change their minds."

I was not going to back down. "If we let them go through with it, we're just as guilty."

Barry snorted, "Well, there's no way out as I see it."

"God will provide a way. He always does. From the time of Cain and Abel, the Flood, throughout the whole history of Israel, He has always provided an alternative to self-destruction."

"You really believe that stuff, don't you?" he asked in an inquisitive way.

"With every fiber of my being," I answered.

"I'd ask how come, but it's probably a dangerous question to ask a preacher. And at this time of night I'm not sure I could hold out for an hour's sermon."

"What if I told you I could answer in two words?" I asked.

"Do it," he answered.

"Jesus and the resurrection."

Instead of questioning me any further, Barry simply said, "That's nice. At least you believe in something."

"I take it you're not a believer," I replied.

"I believe a G sharp is a half note higher than a G natural. I believe f=ma. I believe you can't push a rope. Those are the only three absolutes in my life. Everything else is relative." Barry said this in such a way that he was neither boasting nor feeling sorry for himself. He paused for a moment, as if what he had just said jolted him. He cocked his head as he sat in a rocking chair at the foot of my bed. "How did you get into all this religious stuff anyway? When we roomed together I knew you went to church and all, but I never thought you were so serious you'd devote your life to the church."

"I never thought of it as devoting my life to the church," I answered. "I devoted my life to God. The ministry was the one profession where I could learn more about God and even get paid for it." I chuckled. "I never got paid much, but I always got paid."

The light in the room was soft and dim, but I could make out Barry's features. He seemed puzzled by my statements. "Look," he began, "it's none of my business, but what you've been saying . . . well, it doesn't make a lot of sense to me, O.K.?"

"Which part?" I asked.

"You became a pastor to learn more about God, right?"

"Yes."

"You went through all kinds of training and education, served in little churches, ended up at the last one which started small but grew to eleven hundred?"

"That was the membership, but usually only seven hundred attended."

"Whatever. You had plenty of successful programs?"

"Correct."

"Added on to the church?"

"Right."

"Burned the mortgage?"

"Yes."

"Visited the sick in the hospitals?"

"Yes."

"You were an active force in the community?"

"I'd say so."

"Chairman of the ministerial association in the area?"

"For three years, yes."

"Always faithful to your wife? "

"Of course. Barry, where is this taking us?"

He rocked back and forth very slowly, then leaned forward. "You wonder why I'm not a believer?" he asked. "Why, if I was in that church, I'd worship you. Why would I have to worship God? Why would I want to? All your hard work and God pulls you out of service? Some loving God that is!" He said it with a distaste, a repulsion that shocked me.

It was then, by virtue of Barry's questions and the grace of God, that I began to have the mystery removed from me. In his own accidental way Barry had revealed a sin in my life without knowing he had done so. The church *had* grown, and I *was* working long hours, but it was because I was caught up with the adulation, the reverence, the power, and the majesty directed toward *me,* not God. I had placed myself above Him. I had commanded and demanded respect. The church was no longer God's house, it was mine. Seven hundred people came to my house weekly to adore *me.* I closed my eyes and felt warm tears flow down my cheeks. "God forgive me," I said softly.

"Did I say something wrong?"

"No. To the contrary, you said exactly the right thing," I said as the tears continued to flow.

"You actually sound happy," he said in a confused tone of voice.

"I'm very happy," I said as I wiped my cheeks with the back of my hands.

"This has been a tough day for me," Barry said in a bewildered way. "I'd better not drink coffee tomorrow."

"I'll explain it to you later," I smiled. "It's important for me to tell you what I've done wrong. God is good, Barry. You must believe that for now."

"If you say so," he said.

"Just remember Jesus and the resurrection."

"'Jesus and the resurrection' is four words by the way," he teased. "I knew there was no preacher who wouldn't take twice as much time as allowed. Even you."

I threw the pillow at him and hit him squarely in the face. Instead of throwing it back, he placed it on top of his head like a Davey Crockett hat and rocked back and forth. His cheekbones raised high, and there were slits on either side of his nose where his eyes had once been.

It was at that moment I knew about the strength of a bond between two people. I know it sounds strange to talk about another man this way, but at that moment I loved Barry as much as any human being on this good earth. As he rocked back and forth, I silently asked God for forgiveness and thanked Him for sending Barry Gieselmann into my life.

"Barry," I said softly, "we've got to keep Rich and Lyle from carrying out this crazy bank idea."

"I know," he said. "I think I know a way. Just follow my lead tomorrow." He walked toward the door, turned back at me and said, "Roomie, sometime will you tell me more about Jesus and the resurrection?" He left before I could answer.

The sun arose the next morning with a passion to embrace everything and everyone in Leelanau County. There wasn't a hint of clouds anywhere. It was as if they had been declared illegal, so they all retreated to some remote corner of the sky's attic. The blue of the bay matched the sky so perfectly, I had to strain to make out the horizon separating them. It appeared as though I could jump in the ski boat and continue a path all the way to Heaven itself. I imagined myself doing just that, complete with the details of pulling the boat up to Heaven's gate and seeing the surprised look of the angel sitting on the stoop. "Why are you so shocked?" I would ask him. "I'm guaranteed a place here, and you didn't think much of it when Elijah roared up in a fiery chariot. This is the twentieth century, good fellow. Times are changing. Now be a helpful lad and grab the bowline. I'm not an experienced boater, I borrowed this from a friend in Suttons Bay."

I was shaken from my fantasy by the words "Suttons Bay." I heard footsteps in the kitchen. The aroma of freshly brewed coffee overpowered the soap and shampoo I had used for my morning shower. Even the brilliance of the sun would not let me hide in my room from the challenge I had to face with Rich and Lyle. Prayers of repentance the night before had preoccupied my quiet time with the Lord. I was now being called to breakfast by Lyle, who sounded much too cheerful. My hope was that Barry really did have a plan in mind, or at least an argument Lyle and Rich would heed. I said a prayer for wisdom and guidance as I climbed the steps to the breakfast nook jutting out from the kitchen.

The table was set with china, fine silver, a glass of freshly squeezed orange juice at each place setting. French doors from the breakfast nook to an attached screened-in porch were thrown open. The bay's presence was as dramatic as if a fifth place setting had been put down for it at our table. The shrill cries of distant sea gulls blended with the rhythmic hissing of tiny waves washing the sugar-white sand on the beach beneath us.

"Great morning, isn't it?" asked Lyle as Rich and Barry took their seats at the table. I smiled and nodded yes, preferring to avoid discussing the night before unless someone else forced the issue. Deep in my heart I hoped our discussion would be forgotten. Perhaps at another gathering in the future we would look back at the previous night with a mixture of humor and relief, saved from an idea which could only produce evil. But my wish disappeared as quickly as the clouds that had surrounded us the day before.

"Eat hearty, mates," Lyle said in an English sailor's accent. "We've got a mighty task ahead of us, we do. 'Ere's some heavy planning to be done t'day, and we'll all have to be on top of it. I got some sausages an' biscuits for ye, mates. Even have a spot o' tea in the toddy for you, Barry." Lyle bounced around the table, dishing out food, pouring coffee, acting more energized than at any time since we had been together. It was clear he was not going to forget the previous night. In fact, it seemed to breathe new life into him.

Barry looked squarely at Lyle. "I've been thinking about this little caper," he said. "By the way, is what we're doing called a caper? It is in all the B grade movies."

Lyle rubbed the palms of his hands back and forth with delight. "I've been thinking about it too, and I call it a chance to prove ourselves."

"To whom?" I asked.

"To the most important people in the world—us!" He said this with such an energy level, it was clear he was not going to be dissuaded easily, if at all.

"Right on," mumbled Rich as he stuffed a biscuit in his mouth.

My head snapped as Barry said, "When do we begin planning this thing and stop talking about it?" He looked at Lyle without blinking.

"All right, Gieselmann!" Lyle gushed. "And here I thought you might back out on us. Want some more tea?"

Barry didn't answer, but pushed away from the table and walked to the center-island stove to pour himself another cup. "I don't mean to be plebeian about this robbery, but don't you think it's a little showy to rob the place in a Cadillac limousine?"

"Good point," Rich mumbled as he bit into a sausage.

"We'll work something out," Lyle answered. "We can rent a car in Traverse City."

Barry sipped his tea. "Yeah, that might work. Rich, did you bring a credit card? They won't rent you one if you pay cash."

Rich was ladling jam onto another biscuit. "They won't?" he

asked. "That's un-American. Why do we always have to . . . Hey, I'm not going to use *my* credit card for this thing. I could be traced."

"We could all use bicycles," Barry mused. "Trail bikes maybe. There are some great trails and hills around here. We could rob the bank and take a nice ride through the hills. It would make it even more memorable for us."

Lyle was shaking his head and squinting at Barry. "Look," he said, "let's not sweat the small stuff. For now let's just talk this thing out. We can get down to the fine points later."

"Using my credit card to rent a getaway car isn't small stuff to me," Rich protested.

"Besides, he might be maxed out," Barry said with a straight face. "I always hate how snotty the clerks can be when they tell you the card is maxed out."

"I'm sure as heck not riding any bike to do a bank job," Rich added as he stabbed a sausage with his fork.

"Guys, guys, guys," Lyle said with a less than sincere grin on his face. "We're getting bogged down by picky little details. Let's just keep this on a high plane for a while."

"Something like this can be kept on a high plane as compared to murder and rape which would be sordid by comparison," I blurted out sarcastically.

"I thought we said there would be no violence," mumbled Rich with half a sausage in his mouth.

"Maxing out a credit card can be violent," Barry added. "As they run it through the machine you can hear that sucker hit the wall. That's what makes the kerchunk sound as they run the card through. You know the one I'm talking about? They put the card in the machine, draw it across the card, then the machine goes *kerCHUNK!*" He imitated a clerk running a credit card through. "*KerCHUNK!* That noise is the sound of another card hitting the wall from max-out. *KerCHUNK!* It sounds violent, doesn't it?"

"It doesn't matter anyway," smirked Rich. "They repossessed my credit cards when I got too far behind. We'll have to use someone else's."

"We're not going to use a credit card to rent a getaway car!" Lyle shouted in frustration.

"Well, we better come up with something better than the stupid bike idea then," Rich said as he slurped from his coffee cup.

I could feel the heat of the sun warming the breakfast area. The sun's warmth combined with the hot coffee was causing me to perspire lightly. Lyle, however, was flushed red. Beads of sweat dotted his forehead. He drummed his fingers on the table while shooting icy glances at Barry and Rich each time they spoke.

"First of all, we don't even know the layout of the bank. We've got to stake it out for a while. We've got to position ourselves around town so we can learn all we need to know about the place. This morning I drew a map of the town, including the strategic spots giving us some needed intelligence."

I grunted and rolled my eyes.

Lyle pushed aside the plates, saucers, and silverware as he rolled out a crude pencil drawing of the village on the backside of a roll of Christmas wrapping paper. "Here's the bank," Lyle said, pointing to a penciled rectangle.

"It looks like Santa's belly to me," Barry remarked, his head tilted, a puzzled frown on his face.

Lyle looked at him angrily.

"Oh, I got it now. The light was coming through the paper. Put it flat on the table will you, Lyle? That way the sun can't bleed through." Barry sounded serious. He even helped Lyle spread the paper across the table, anchoring each corner with a plate of sausages, a marmalade jar, a dish of butter, and a half-drunk cup of tea.

Rich and Barry flanked Lyle on each side, while I sat in a chair at the table pretending to be uninterested in the conversation. Lyle sketched more details onto the map with a felt-tipped marker. The excitement in his voice was unmistakable. He spoke with an infectious enthusiasm as he described streets and stores in the area of the bank. "Directly across from the bank is a series of shops with a good flow of traffic. We could station ourselves at these places throughout the day without anyone getting suspicious. The places with the best views of the bank are Jon's Barber Shop and Fish Tackle Store, a grocery store, and a funeral home."

"I don't like the sound of those places for surveillance," Barry said seriously.

"Why not?" Lyle asked.

"If we send Rich into a barber shop, everyone in town will get suspicious."

"I have to get my hair cut just like you guys," Rich pouted.

"Not really," Barry countered, "we get the top cut too." He rubbed Rich's bald head with the palm of his hand to show he was only joking. "We could send you to the funeral home though. I hope you feel better than you look."

"I'm never drinking again," Rich said sadly. "The first reason is because it makes me feel terrible, and second because we're out of beer. I'll bet I could pass as a customer at the funeral home the way I feel today."

Lyle shut off the jovial exchange. "I'll make the assignments around here until we have more data to work with," he said in an authoritative voice. "Here's how we'll start this morning. We'll split up and walk around the town like any other fudgie tourists. Stop in the souvenir shops, get an ice cream cone, stroll around taking pictures, go to the art galleries and antique stores looking at everything, browse through the clothes stores fingering the merchandise—don't do anything to draw suspicion. By noon we meet back here. Each of us will have a specific assignment to report at lunchtime. Ron, I want you to visit the barber shop. Wait until a crowd gathers in the shop and sit there listening to what they talk about. Notice the traffic in and out of the bank."

"Won't I look a little conspicuous just hanging around a barber shop?" I asked.

"Get your hair cut while you're there," Lyle remarked. "You're starting to look a little seedy anyway. If you don't want to get your hair cut, ask to look at the fishing tackle."

"I don't know how to fish," I said.

"Well, you know how to grow hair, so I guess it's haircut time," Lyle answered with a sneer.

He gave Barry and Rich their assignments without asking whether or not I was willing to participate. Rich was to park his truck in the bank's lot and walk across the street to the grocery store for a new supply of food and beer. He was also to take note of any special traffic patterns such as cash deliveries made to the bank by armored trucks or local businesses. Barry was the only one who would actually go into the bank itself, asking if he could cash an out-of-state check. Lyle gave him orders to wait until the cashier lines were long. Barry could survey the bank's layout including the placement of the tellers, the manager, and the vault. While we were in town, Lyle was going to find out the routes of the county sheriff and local law enforcement agencies for both day and night. He would also determine how many patrol cars were in service during the weekdays and on weekends so we could do the job when there were the lowest number of cars on duty.

I loudly protested the idea of what we were doing. Lyle, however, was so enchanted by the thrill of the challenge, he sloughed my concerns aside saying we were only thinking about the possibilities, and no decisions had been made yet. I could tell he was lying again. Rich, too, was eager. It was clear he and Lyle had already made up their minds to go through with this foolishness regardless of the consequences. I regretted not being more convincing. Soon I would be forced to make several difficult choices; none were appealing to me. There was no way I could participate in a robbery, yet I didn't want to leave without doing my utmost to foil the attempt. If I did leave, I had the unenviable choice of informing the police or becoming an accessory to the crime by not informing them. Sometime soon I was going to have to talk with Barry about how he intended to prevent this stupidity from becoming reality. If he had a plan in mind, it was less than apparent. He seemed to be going along with Lyle and Rich, offering no visible resistance. In fact, it was Barry who asked for a clarification of our assignments. Lyle repeated them again, slowly and carefully.

Lyle summed our breakfast up by saying, "This is just a scouting trip this morning. See what you can pick up. Don't look obvious about anything. We'll meet back here for lunch and talk about what we've got."

"Sounds good to me," said Barry. He looked at me and winked as Rich and Lyle headed out the door. Only God and Barry knew for sure what was behind the wink. And only God knew what was beyond the wink.

FOURTEEN

I walked around the streets of Suttons Bay for nearly two hours debating with myself whether I should even comply with Lyle's order about visiting the barber shop. While I was never able to completely forget the mission I was on, the charm of this little village captured my imagination to sufficiently distract me from the bizarre idea of robbing a bank. The village reminded me of a little plastic town my brother and I would build to place alongside the tracks of our electric trains. While many of the storefronts were façades placed on older buildings, each façade was meticulously painted, the windows decorated with flower boxes of red geraniums, yellow marigolds, or pink and white impatiens. Park benches were strategically placed along the sidewalks to provide a view of the bay or serve as resting places beneath canvas awnings hanging from the storefronts in colorful disarray like a medley of flags at the United Nations. Each store window boasted a simple display of just enough goods to entice visitors to come inside and browse.

I had enough time to stroll to the marina and beach. Neither would have been out of place on a picture postcard. From the vantage point of a small knoll, the beach and marina seemed to form a large script W. The left loop on the W was the beach. It was occupied by more sunbathers than swimmers. A lifeguard sitting on a tall, white platform chair spun a silver whistle around her finger in lazy loops while two little children splashed each other at the water's edge.

The right side of the W was lined with sail- and powerboats.

The boats were tied to narrow wooden catwalks supported by metal pipes screwed into the sandy floor of the bay. Judging by people getting in and out of their boats, the catwalks did not provide steady footing. I noticed only smaller boats were tied to the catwalks. The bigger ones were placed along a cement wall on the peninsula portion of the W. Space for larger boats was limited, it seemed, as several were anchored further out, with people traversing to and from shore by way of dinghies. At the lower end of the right loop of the W was a three-story condominium complex painted barn-red. It looked like it had been transplanted from somewhere in New England. Small, wooden decks holding chaise lounges and patio settees jutted out from each of the condo units. One couple sitting on a second-story deck ignored the activity at the marina and the beach alike. The woman, still in her bathrobe, was watching a soap opera on a portable TV, while her husband read a newspaper with his feet propped on the deck's top railing.

I reluctantly left the marina area and made my way back toward the barber shop. By the time I got there, every waiting chair was filled, and tourists were wandering in and out. I found this surprising since there seems to be little browsing one can do in a barber shop, even if it does sell fishing tackle too. Neither the barber nor any of the others waiting seemed bothered by the strangers or my presence. Still, I felt conspicuous, as if everyone knew I was there to watch the activity in the bank across the street. I was relieved when a waiting chair came open, as the chairs faced away from the bank and I would be able to report very little to Lyle at lunch. Somehow this seemed to do my conscience some good, but I knew I had to get more aggressive if Lyle and Rich were to be stopped. The conversation in the barber shop centered around sudden changes in the weather, how lousy the Tigers were playing, how lousy the sport fishing was since the native Americans were allowed to use gill nets, what a person could do with the money from winning the state lottery, and how cheap a local restaurant had been for not supporting the Little League by taking out an ad in their program. The bank was never mentioned. For all you could tell from the conversation it didn't even exist.

I was delighted. I had learned nothing. Perhaps time would be my ally in foiling the idiocy we were contemplating. Rich's fiancée would be with us in three more days, and the wedding would take place as soon as the AIDS instruction classes and licensing requirements were completed. If we were all thwarted from learning anything about the bank and its operation, perhaps time would be able to save us from ourselves. I left the shop with a fresh haircut and absolutely no more knowledge about the bank than when I had left the house three hours earlier. Never before had I ever been so happy to be so dumb.

I half walked, half jogged back to the house, delighted with the notion that if each of us was unable to learn anything significant about the bank's operations, we would have to abandon the plan. Lyle was probably the one person who would come back with information, but it would be a useless piece of a jigsaw puzzle if Rich, Barry, and I came back empty-handed. I was surprised I hadn't seen either Rich or Barry all morning long. While the town was dotted with stores, galleries, and tourist attractions, they nearly all fronted on either side of the one main street curving through the village. It seemed inevitable that four people would have to cross paths at some moment within a three-hour time span, yet I never saw any one of the others.

As I approached the house, I saw Rich's Toyota truck in the driveway with his legs sticking out of the window of the passenger door. His high-top sneakers were untied in the currently fashionable way, and the only movement was from his shoelaces swaying gently from the push of soft bay breezes. Each foot was solidly immobile, and I panicked at the thought that something foul had happened to Rich. My pulse quickened as I sprinted to the driver's door of the truck, fearing I might see Rich bloodied and battered. He was clearly unconscious, mouth open, with drool running out one corner and down his cheek. His right arm flopped lazily at a 90 degree angle, with his hand resting on his stomach, his left arm extending down to the truck's floorboard where an open-palmed left hand rested among four empty beer cans. I opened the driver's door quickly, Rich did not move. His eyes rolled back at me, unfocused and bloodshot.

"S'zat you, Ron?" he slurred.

"Rich, what happened?" I asked. It didn't seem like a silly question at the time, but in retrospect my naiveté was surfacing again.

"Be darned if I know," he said as he groggily pulled himself into an upright position. "I got kinda bored in town, so after I picked up the groceries and some beer, I thought I'd come here to see the pretty view and wait for you guys. I had a couple of beers, and it's all I remember."

I didn't see any groceries. "Where is the food you bought?" I asked him.

"Isn't it here?" he answered. He checked the cab, then turned to look into the truck's empty bed. "Maybe I forgot it. I might have left it at the store."

"Do you remember buying food?" I asked.

"Don't remember," he mumbled.

Lyle pulled up in the white Cadillac limo. He was smiling as he bounded up to the truck, where his smile vanished. "What's going on?" he said with more of a tone of accusation than inquiry.

"Don't remember," Rich mumbled again.

"You've been drinking," Lyle growled.

"Only had a couple," Rich sniffed. "I just fell asleep is all. I'll be all right."

"I hope so. I got some key information this morning. There's a window of time that would work out for us just dandy. I'll go in and get lunch started. I want to compare what I've learned with what you three picked up this morning." He spun on his heel and headed straight for the house, bouncing energetically on the balls of his feet as he walked.

Rich sat in the cab of his truck staring blankly out the windshield. "Did you learn a lot this morning?" he asked numbly.

"Not much," I replied, although I was learning more by the minute. "How about you?"

"Don't remember," he mumbled. "Lyle will get mad at me. People get mad when I can't remember."

"Let's just wait out here for a while," I said. "Maybe things will start to come back to you."

"Maybe," he said with no expression. "Maybe." He fumbled around on the floor of the truck until he found a full can of beer amidst the empties. He popped the can and drank from it in big gulps. "Aaahhhhh. Yeah, I remember now. I do. I remember." He looked at me with wide, moist eyes. "We're gonna rob a bank," he said sloppily as he put his hand alongside my cheek.

Not with my help, I thought as Lyle called us in for lunch.

Rich brought another can of beer into the house and popped it open as we sat down to eat. Lyle watched Rich carefully at first, but ignored him after five minutes or so. He turned his attention instead to Barry, who hadn't come back yet. Rich had wisely chosen not to talk since Lyle's mood was becoming angrier the longer Barry was away. The alcohol was taking Rich away mentally, and he would have incurred Lyle's wrath, which was directed at me instead.

"What's keeping him?" Lyle fired at me.

"How should I know?" I teased.

"You roomed with him. You two were talking last night about something. Where is he?"

I tried to sound calm, but I remembered Barry had threatened to leave, and it occurred to me he might have done so. "Lyle, I roomed with Barry twenty years ago. We talked last night, but it wasn't about where he would be at lunchtime today. Why are you so anxious? If he's late for lunch, he'll have to eat the food cold. That was the rule my mother had."

"Well, I'm not your mother," he growled. "I've got some great information, but it's got to fit with what the three of you picked up this morning."

Rich looked a little pale. He said he had to use the bathroom. I also excused myself to check Barry's room. To my surprise, his clothes appeared to be there, his bed was neatly made, and an open Bible was lying on the headrest of the bed. I picked up the Bible. It was opened to Luke 24. Carefully placing the Bible back in its original position, I marveled at how God works, then returned upstairs to Lyle and Ron.

"I yum not drung," I heard Rich protesting.

"You're bombed!" Lyle said in a menacing tone. "We've got important business to take care of and you're bombed!"

"Gotta go to the bathroom," Rich grumbled.

"You just went to the bathroom," Lyle argued.

"Well, I don't remember going. An' I gotta go again. Don' forget it either. I don' remember so good when I been drinkin'."

"So you admit you're bombed," Lyle chanted like a district attorney.

"Did I say that? I don' remember saying that. You said that. Y' know Lyle, I don' talk so good when I been drinkin', but you don' listen too good when I been drinkin'. An' I admit I have been drinkin', but I'm not bombed." Rich took two steps toward the bathroom and fell flat on his face.

"Help him. We've got to help him," I hollered to Lyle.

"You've got to be kidding me," he scoffed. "There's nothing we can do for him. Let him lay there and sleep it off."

"Let's at least put him on a couch or bed," I said.

"O.K., let's put him on a chaise lounge on the rear deck. The fresh air might do him some good."

Rich was not a big man, but I was surprised how much trouble Lyle and I had lifting and carrying him onto the rear deck. As we struggled with Rich, I could sense the anger in Lyle rising to the surface. He gritted his teeth as we grunted our way along. Rich groaned once as we flopped him onto the lounge. Lyle stood over him, shaking his head back and forth in disgust.

I used the quiet moment as an opening. "Lyle, let's abandon this bank idea. Rich obviously has a problem, and I really didn't find out anything useful this morning."

"Yeah, well, that's your problem. Let me tell you what I learned. It's dynamite! The county sheriff has an outdated radio communications system. It can only project and receive in a limited range. The patrol cars have a regular pattern they follow, checking in with each other by radio every fifteen minutes. They talk to each other or the dispatcher, who relays messages if they're important."

"This sounds confusing, Lyle."

"Let me finish, let me finish," he said impatiently. "There's a period of time between 10 P.M. and 10:30 where the cars and the dispatcher can't talk to each other because of the lousy equipment. One car passes by the bank shortly after 10. That means there's a window of opportunity of about twenty-five minutes where we could get into the place without having every cop in the county on our trail."

"Lyle, what good would it do if we get into the bank at night? The money must be locked up somewhere."

"Great thinking, Ron," he said sarcastically. "My guess is it's in a vault. That's why banks put them there. To hold money."

"And they can't be penetrated unless you know how to pick the locks. Do you know how to do that? This isn't the same as breaking into a Cadillac with its keys locked in the ignition, you know."

"I thought you Christian types were possibility thinkers," he sneered. "If there's more than one way to skin a cat, there's more than one way to open a vault. Come with me."

He led me around the house to a storage area beneath the deck where Rich was sleeping. Hand tools, two half-inflated rubber beach rafts, an old lawn mower, and a strange array of coffee cans and glass jars holding screws, bolts, nails, and washers were stuffed into the storage space with no pattern or order. The storage area was cool despite the noonday heat because the lower level was built into the side of a hill.

"Right over here," Lyle said nearly in a whisper. He placed one foot delicately over a garden rake, stepped around the lawn mower, then pushed one of the beach rafts aside. The raft knocked over a coffee can filled with finishing nails, sending it to the floor with a crash. Lyle froze to a dead stop. He exhaled a big sigh, kneeled down in one corner, and lifted up a metal box secured by a cheap tumbler lock. Lyle opened the lock with a few quick spins and brought the box over to me. Inside was a small pancake-like object wrapped in what I thought was wax paper.

"Here's our secret weapon," Lyle whispered.

"It's very nice, Lyle, but I'm full from lunch and couldn't eat another bite."

"You don't know what this is, do you?" he asked in a hushed, mocking tone.

"What ever it is, it has taken your voice away," I said, mocking him in return.

"It's plastic explosives. Used by terrorists and unethical construction crews around the world."

"Oh, oh. Where did you . . ."

"When Mirkin was building this place, the contractor had to clear away a portion of this bluff. Plastic explosives are illegal, I think. The Department of Natural Resources won't issue a soil erosion permit if you use any, that's for sure. I watched the crew use it. It's quite simple actually. A small detonating device, even an alarm clock or radio signal, can set it off. A couple wads of this stuff carefully placed on the door of the vault and we can walk into it like Sherman took Atlanta. I think I can make it work."

I shuddered. Plastic explosives had been in the news just recently. They were identified as an illegal industry of the overthrown Czech government. An airliner was blown up over Scotland by plastic explosives, a terrorist group planted them in a sidewalk cafe filled with tourists, and a nightclub in Germany frequented by American GIs had been leveled by them. Now Lyle was talking about adding one more crime to the list. Plastics were no longer something remote and distant. They were close enough to impact my own life. My face felt like it was on fire, my shirt clung to the small of my back, my hands were numb, and I suddenly had trouble breathing.

"I've got to get some air," I croaked. I dashed outside and sucked in the warm bay breeze with deep gasps. The prospect of being involved had escalated beyond the mere thinking and joking stage. Lyle was serious. Deadly serious.

He emerged from the storage space, locked it, walked beside me, and put an arm around my shoulder. "This is exciting stuff, isn't it? I haven't been this turned on in years."

I turned away without making a comment. In the corner of my eye I thought I saw some movement in the house. I looked up on the deck. Barry was standing there looking down on us. His arms were folded across his chest, and he rocked back and forth on his heels. A broad grin covered his face, his eyes had disappeared into tiny slits. He looked as if he had discovered something neither of us had known. As usual, he was right.

FIFTEEN

She was not so much beautiful as she was striking. Her black ballet slipper shoes were laced in a criss-cross pattern around calves shaded by black nylons. The laces of the shoes wound all the way to the ruffled hem of her skirt. The skirt itself was a floral pattern of reds, yellows, and blues, with a green vine winding its way through the flowers in a quiet, subtle way. The white peasant blouse she wore had a wide boat neck clearly revealing five or six necklaces of various lengths. Her black hair was pulled back over her ears where long, gold, circular earrings hung. She smelled like fresh peach blossoms. An easy smile crossed her face, as if strangers were only friends she hadn't met yet. My first impression was she looked very much like a Gypsy. Despite her puffy clothes it was clear she was quite thin, with an angular face accented by high cheekbones and a pointed chin.

Barry stood beside her in the kitchen as Lyle and I entered. He had a smirk on his face that was difficult to read. I took it to mean he was pleased with himself. Lyle did not look happy, but said nothing until the introductions were completed.

"This is Myra," Barry said as he pointed to each of us by name.

"Hi, Lyle. Hi, Ron. This is a lovely place you have," she said breezily to neither of us in particular.

"Thank you," Lyle answered quickly.

"It belongs to Lyle's boss," Barry told her.

Lyle grimaced, but didn't disagree with Barry.

"Maybe you know him," Barry continued. "His name is Mirkin."

"Oh, the Mirkins. Sure, I know them. They come into the store a lot during the season."

"The store?" I asked.

"Yes. I work at the department store in the village. We carry a complete line of clothes. The whole family shops there."

"Where's Rich?" Barry asked.

"Sleeping on the back deck," I indicated with a nod of my head.

"Last night too much for him?" Barry asked with a grin.

"So, Barry, what brings you and Myra around?" Lyle questioned in a manner suggesting he was tired of the small talk.

"She said she has been by the place a number of times and always wanted to know what the inside looks like."

"I hope you don't mind," she said politely to Lyle. She put her hand on his forearm, and he looked down at it. He didn't seem to mind her touch; in fact, he looked pleased.

"Of course not," he said lamely. "Happy to have guests. Barry can show you around."

"Do you rent this from the Mirkins?" she asked.

"I'm a friend of the family," Lyle answered.

"Lyle's a handy guy to have around," Barry said flatly.

Lyle flinched slightly, and I thought he had taken Barry's remark as an insult. His next statement verified my suspicion. "Myra . . . What a pretty name. It doesn't sound foreign."

"Myra isn't a foreign name, but I was born in Armenia. How did you know?" She seemed genuinely impressed with Lyle's perception.

"Lucky guess," he said. Lyle looked at Barry and said, "Your record is still intact."

"Seriously," she said, grabbing Lyle's hand, "how could you tell? I've worked so hard to avoid an accent. Could you hear an accent or what?"

This time Lyle did look uncomfortable by her touch. She did not let go of his hand right away, not because she was making an overture toward him, but because she seemed to be the kind of person who touched others naturally and did not think it unusual.

"It must be wonderful to work in this part of the country," I interjected, hoping to ease Lyle's anxious look.

She released Lyle's hand as she answered. "It's all right. I would rather work fewer hours, but there's a saying up here that 'Half the pay is the view of the bay,' and it's true. I've got to work three jobs just to make ends meet. But I'm not the only one. Almost everyone who lives here year-round has the same situation."

Barry spoke up merrily. "Myra and I are going out to dinner tonight. Do you mind if I borrow the limo, Lyle? Boy, that sounds like a line out of my teens. Instead of 'Dad, can I borrow the car?' it's 'Lyle can I borrow the limo?'" He chuckled, enjoying his little joke.

"We have some things to discuss this evening. Remember?" Lyle said stiffly.

"Ah, Dad, errrr, Lyle, I promise I'll be home early."

"Take it," Lyle grumbled. "Just don't bang it up. I could get in trouble."

"You're very kind," Myra said. She put her arm inside Lyle's and squeezed it gently.

Lyle winced and actually blushed. She was so carefree, so giving of herself that I thought at first he might think she was trying to seduce him. Instead of admitting he liked her attention and company, Lyle did just the opposite—he turned hostile. His entire tone was unkind and bitter.

"What do you do besides work at the department store?" Lyle asked with a sneer.

"I sell tickets at the movie theater in the winter, also work at the art gallery where I met Barry and . . ."

"I didn't want your life story," interrupted Lyle.

"Maybe I should show Myra around," Barry said as he took her by the elbow.

"Why not, Gieselmann," Lyle sighed. "I ask you to do one simple thing today and you can't get it right. Don't make any wrong turns as you go through the house."

Barry looked undaunted. He leaned close to Lyle and whispered, "Lyle, I did just what you asked. I went to town and picked up what I could."

Myra looked at her watch and touched Barry on the back of the arm. "I don't mean to rush, but I've got to be back in a half hour," she said.

"Another job to go to, I'll bet," Lyle smirked.

She looked at him in amazement. She walked directly to him, picked up both his hands in hers. "Lyle, I'd like to learn more about you sometime. I think you really are psychic. I'm interested in the occult myself."

"I'll bet you are," he sneered as he pulled his hand out from hers. "Is that your afternoon job? Telling fortunes at the yogurt stand?"

This time Lyle had gone too far. There was no subtlety in what he said, or the way he had said it. Myra's dark brown eyes flashed at his insults.

"Lyle . . ." I began, but was interrupted.

"I was wrong," she flared. "I don't need to know any more about you. This afternoon, down at the marina, I'll clean a couple of condos with my brother who has a cleaning service. It's one of three jobs he holds also. Then, after dinner with Barry my brother and I will clean the bank in town where arrogant jerks like you put their money so fools like me can earn a living."

"The bank across from the barber shop?" Lyle gasped.

"It's the only one in town. I thought a know-it-all like you would have figured that out." She was still angry, but seemed to be cooling off given Lyle's more civil approach.

Lyle put on the charm, as I had seen him do with us. "Please forgive me, Myra," he said humbly. "I've acted badly. Barry may have told you, but in case he hasn't, I lost my wife a short while back, and I'm still a little uneasy . . ."

"Oh, I'm so sorry," she said. She put her hand to his face.

"Actually I admire people who work hard." He was almost whispering. "I didn't mean to sound so rude." He took her hand and held it between both of his. "Both you and your brother sound like the kind of people I most admire."

"I'm sorry too," she said with a touch of sadness in her voice. "I didn't mean to snap at you."

"Perhaps I could make it up to you by having you and your brother over here for a drink after work. Or perhaps a boat ride when you're finished?"

She laughed. "That's very kind, but we don't get started until 10, 10:15 at night, and we're not done until midnight or one o'clock, depending on whether we wash the inside windows or not."

Lyle lifted her hand and kissed it. "Myra, you are a dear, dear person. Please accept my apologies with an assurance you are welcome here whenever you like."

Lyle turned to Barry and handed him the keys to the limo. "Take Myra back after you've shown her through the house, Barry. You've both added so much to my day. Letting you use the car is the least I can do in return."

Lyle walked out of the room and winked at me as he walked by.

"All right, Gieselmann!" Lyle gushed as Barry entered the house from his return of Myra. Lyle slapped Barry on the back as if he had just won an Olympic gold medal. "And to think I doubted you," crooned Lyle.

"Yeah, I'm good, aren't I?" Barry responded.

Rich stumbled into the kitchen from his afternoon siesta. "What did you do, Barry?" he asked.

"Nothing. How are you feeling?" Barry replied.

"Such modesty. He got the keys to the bank is what he did!" Lyle crowed.

Rich opened the refrigerator door as he scratched his stomach. "I'm kinda thirsty. We have anything to drink?"

Lyle reached in front of Rich and slammed the door shut. "Yeah, water. You take it from the tap. Your drinking days are over until we do this bank job. It's going to be tough enough with all of us sober. We don't need a drunk to complicate matters."

Rich looked hurt. He acted as if he was going to protest Lyle's statement, but turned to the cupboards, took out a glass, and filled it with water instead. Rich mumbled, "I still don't know what happened."

"Barry, the genius, found us a way to get into the bank without any pain or fuss. Rich, when we were in school, who did you think was the smartest person in the world?" asked an enthused Lyle.

"Einstein," Rich mumbled.

Lyle chided, "Not in the whole world, just in our world. The smartest, most talented person you had to deal with on a day to day basis."

Rich looked confused. "I guess that eliminates Einstein then, doesn't it? I don't know, Lyle. The smartest and most talented..."

"It was Gieselmann!" Lyle shouted as he wrapped his arm around Barry's shoulder. "He was the smartest, most talented guy then, and he still is."

"Barry?" Rich asked incredulously. "You think Barry was smarter than Einstein?"

Lyle didn't slow down one bit. It was as if he was negotiating with car dealers again, feasting on compliments and smooth talk, starving for anything of substance. "Smarter and better-looking both. Barry has shown us how the relationship between time and ultimate achievement can be cut in half in the wink of an eye... Or at least by the presence of a Gypsy cleaning woman."

"Have I been asleep for a long time?" Rich asked me seriously. "I don't remember a lot of what Lyle is talking about."

"Not to worry, little fella," Lyle said as he rubbed Rich's bald head. "You and I are going to practice making booming noises with a little nutty putty this afternoon. Your work as a handyman will be just what we need to manufacture a plastic key that vaults us into showing the world we can do whatever we put our minds to. That's a little play on words, get it? 'Vaults us into.'"

Rich looked totally bewildered. Lyle dropped his arm from Barry's shoulder and wrapped it around Rich's instead. They walked out of the kitchen toward the front door. Lyle shouted over his shoulder, "We'll be back by six o'clock. If you guys leave, make sure you lock the door. I wouldn't want anyone to break in." Lyle laughed as he and Rich made their way to the storage area, then down the road in the white limousine.

SIXTEEN

The masks of comedy and tragedy were personified by the contrast between Lyle and Barry. Barry was as depressed as Lyle was pleased with the discovery of Myra. For several minutes after Lyle and Rich had left, Barry stood motionless by the windows, staring at the bay. Bright sunlight flooded the area, and the bay was active with boaters and swimmers who could be clearly seen but not heard. The world outside seemed to be so free of cares, a place to frolic in crystal blue water and bright sun. Inside we were wrestling with the darkness of a crime which was designed in a moment of weakness, but had grown like a Frankenstein monster.

I pretended to busy myself around the house, although Barry was never out of my sight. He didn't move, and to a casual passerby he might have looked like a store window mannequin. I asked him several times if he wanted to go for a walk, but he did not respond in any way. He merely stood by the windows, staring blankly at a scene of natural grandeur whose beauty had been robbed from him by the vanity and weakness of Man. He was physically immobile, and I felt emotionally unable to help him out of the torment he was feeling. Instinctively I prayed to God for wisdom and mercy, coming to grips once again with my own frailty and ineptness in a time of crisis.

This incident was so typical of my life. When all seemed to be going well, I was quick to take full credit for the success. When trouble was at my doorstep, however, I called upon the Lord for help. As I prayed now, I was struck by how similar Lyle and I were. Driven by a need to succeed, Lyle was willing to go to any lengths to show what he was capable of doing. My own needs were more subtle, and therefore more devious through their subtlety. Many of my pastoral duties were carried out so my congregation would see in me the person of Christ, not for His glory, but for my own. My dismissal from the pastorate was not over great theological issues as much as it was from my alignment with a group within the church who wanted to redirect how God should be worshiped. They played to my vanity, and I was foolish enough to be ensnared. Instead of seeking what God would want for the church, I aligned myself with a faction who knew how to make my ego float, who saw me as a tool to be used, who tempted me with nothing more than my own arrogance about the true and proper way God should be worshiped. Not once did I call upon the Lord for ways He could be made more relevant to the entire church body. I had determined (through the well-meaning advice of others) how He would be worshiped. I looked at resistance to my ideas as Satan-inspired.

What I failed to see then, but was becoming so clear to me in retrospect, was how God did not need my help—He needed my obedience. I had thought of myself as sacrificing for Him—and in my own mind and in the view of most people, I was sacrificing for Him. My family had barely known me over the past two years. Diane was pursuing her career with vigor as much from my own neglect as from her own initiative. My daughter had passed from a delight to an enigma. I counted her distance from me as part of my sacrifice for the Lord. My only failing in these sacrifices was obedience to Him.

How clear this seemed to me now. How foolish I had been. Yet I approached the future, even the misery of what we were encountering, with a renewed spirit because of God's promises, because of my faith in all He had been and would continue to be.

As I prayed I became aware of sounds from the piano. Barry was playing *Fur Elise* by Beethoven. A simple song, it was one I might never have recognized except through my association with

Barry. He told me it was one of the first songs he had committed to memory, and whenever he felt lost or misdirected, he returned to *Fur Elise* because of its simplicity. He played the entire piece three times in a row, while I sat in a chair silently listening to the delicacy with which he played. At the end of the third playing, he carefully pulled down the cover for the keys and slid it over them. He stood, placed the piano bench beneath the keyboard, ran the fingers of his right hand across the wooden music shelf, then lowered the lid on the piano slowly, letting it drop the final two inches so it closed with a loud thud.

We took a long walk to the marina. Conversation did not seem relevant at the time, and I was grateful neither of us tried to force it. I was too busy with my own thoughts to have been a good listener. What Barry was thinking at the time I don't know, but his athletic body was churning. His walking pace was so fast I was hard pressed to keep up with him, let alone carry on an intelligent conversation.

When we reached the marina, we walked out to the furthest point on the peninsula. The grassy finger separating the boating area from the beach served as a launching point for a conversation meaning even more to me today than it did then, though even then I thought of it as a milestone in my life. What Barry had contained inside himself was let out with a near-explosion. With no prompting on my part he began by saying he thought bringing Myra to the house would help confound the bank plan idea. His sole intent was to use her as a complication. Instead she turned out to be an asset in Lyle's evil web, and now Barry feared for Myra's safety. In Barry's estimation, Lyle was off the deep end, and thus beyond convincing through logical persuasion. Now two innocent bystanders, Myra and her brother, could be caught in Lyle's sociopathic scheme through Barry's mistake. He was distraught, without any clear remedies for the problem. With Myra's safety at stake, leaving was no longer an option for him. Alerting the police was premature since there was nothing but idle talk to tell them about.

Barry tried to skip stones out onto the bay as he talked, but was meeting with no success. The small round pebbles he pitched merely hit the surface with a loud plopping sound and sank into the clear blue water. As each stone sank, he threw the next one harder with the same result. His frustration level grew dramatically; perspiration broke out on his forehead. The small of his back became so wet, his knit shirt clung to him like a slimy second skin. Finally he took an entire fist full of stones and threw them into the bay like pellets from a shotgun shell.

From this outburst he poured out his life with a gush of words I can't remember in full detail. What was stunning was the depth and force of emotion he displayed as he played his life out before me. Financial worries had plagued him, not because he wanted for anything specific, but because at forty-three years of age he felt there should be more to life than worrying about making rent payments without stalling on other bills. Nothing he had tried amounted to anything except frustration and disappointment. Being an almost Olympic hopeful was hollow. Failing at even going out on a concert tour was agony. The future was nothing more than an endless repetition of today's failures multiplied by desperation. Even his attempt at thwarting the bank robbery idea ended in failure.

I'm afraid you might think me callous when you hear my reactions to the next part of Barry's story. Indulge me for a while when you hear what I did, for it still confounds me today. Barry admitted he had just stopped hating Lyle before this reunion. He was looking forward to putting the hate behind him when the bank robbery idea got out of control. While I knew something had been eating at Barry, I was shocked he harbored such ill will toward Lyle, let alone that it had been going on for twenty years. I asked what Lyle had done to cause such deep feelings on Barry's part. I had suspected Lyle's mannerisms got under Barry's skin, yet I never thought Barry took what Lyle said or did very seriously. Once, in the quiet of our room during our college years, Barry even admitted he admired Lyle's forcefulness, his brash self-confidence, daring the world to swing at the chin he stuck out before it. Beyond this small admiration I was fairly certain Lyle was both tolerated and ignored by Barry. Instead I learned Barry hated him.

In his senior year Barry was dating a French girl whose parents had sent her to the States to study. Barry was falling in love with her when Lyle asked her out. Barry was sure Lyle did this just to make him angry. She dated Lyle three or four times afterward, but never went out with Barry again. The reason for this was quite clear—Barry never asked her to go out with him again. He turned his back on her and hated Lyle at the same time.

Barry had never met anyone since with the same appeal as that French woman. For twenty years he had blamed his life without marriage on Lyle. It sounds illogical, I know. What is even more preposterous was that Barry never talked to Lyle or the French student about his feelings. While he wiped both from his life, he wiped neither from his memory.

When he finished telling me this part of his life, I did something very unprofessional but marvelously human. I laughed. I roared until tears ran down my cheeks. Barry had just told me the most gut-wrenching episode of his entire life, yet I nearly fell into the bay as I rolled on the grassy ground of the marina's peninsula. In a little while he too was laughing, although he didn't seem to know why. I think he was laughing at me for laughing at him, but at any rate the two of us were coughing and holding our sides, having shared one of the saddest tales that existed between us. When we finished laughing, Barry asked me what we had just found so funny. This sent us into another gale of giggles.

I fear you might think me unfeeling, but Barry's story was typical of so many I had heard. The person who is hated never knows the anger directed his way; meanwhile, the injured party bears all the agony. Barry Gieselmann, the most gifted person I knew, had allowed himself to be emotionally shackled by Lyle Fortrain. It was all so sardonic, so brilliantly evil—Satan himself had clearly mixed human pride with his own noxious fumes.

I apologized to Barry for my behavior and assured him God could deliver us from both Lyle and the Devil if we kept the faith. This caused him to ask again about Jesus and the resurrection. I explained there were times when I had doubts about the behavior of some people in the Bible—the servants of Abraham as Isaac was being led up the mountain, the followers of Christ who disappeared during the crucifixion. But the resurrection kept me from ever doubting God's power or Jesus as His Son. Despite his recent outburst Barry was a logical, scientifically minded, highly disciplined person who needed facts, figures, and reasoning to be convinced about most topics. I explained the chief reference for my belief was the Bible, but I had done some research and found that neither Jew nor Roman during Christ's time had written an account denying the resurrection story. With all the negative sentiments in existence about the Savior, it was amazing that there were no documented records contradicting the Bible's account of what had happened. I could see this made an impression on him, and he asked me questions about Jesus all the way back to the house.

Barry was willing to admit he had sinned. What he couldn't seem to get past was why Christ would be willing to accept a person who had done nothing with his life to merit God's love. While Barry was willing to acknowledge his talents, he was even quicker to despise himself for not achieving anything meaningful with the gifts he had been given. The teasing by Lyle was mild compared to Barry's own self-criticism. He could not understand how God could forgive him for squandering his life so meaninglessly.

Grace, mercy, and unconditional love were mere concepts to Barry. I tried to explain them to the best of my ability. I must confess I am not as effective at evangelistic matters as I would like to be, and I really didn't know if I was making headway with him or not. It wouldn't be until the next morning when Barry called me "brother" that I would know for certain he had turned his life over to Christ. His decision impacted his life and mine in a way that will stay with me for as long as I live. But I am getting ahead of my story.

SEVENTEEN

K aBOOM!" Rich shouted as he came into the house. "You should see this stuff, guys! It can blow a tree stump fifty feet in the air!"

Lyle was trailing behind Rich with a big smile on his face. He didn't see Rich slide a beer out of the refrigerator and slip it into his pants pocket. In fact, in a time span of less than twenty minutes Rich managed to smuggle eight beers out of the refrigerator without any of the rest of us knowing it. Conveniently busying himself while the three of us talked, Rich had a cache of unopened cans neatly cooled in the tanks of toilets throughout the house.

"Our man did some really neat work," Lyle gloated as he put an arm around Rich's shoulder. "We've got this plastic explosive stuff down to a science. If we get any better, we might get recruited by a Lebanese terrorist group."

"KaBOOM!" Rich repeated. He opened the refrigerator door again, pulled out a slice of cheese, then gulped it down in three bites. "The stuff is amazing. It doesn't take but a little spit wad of it and an alarm clock to make a hole in the ground three feet deep. It's so powerful it's scary. I gotta go to the can."

Lyle was moving around the house like a person on videotape in the fast forward position. He rummaged through drawers of tools, opened and closed closet doors, sprinted up and down stairs several times. He finally flopped in a large overstuffed chair in the great room where Barry and I were watching him with suspicious curiosity.

Rich was upstairs in the kitchen when Lyle called to him. "Rich, you want to go with me to Traverse City to pick up some supplies tonight?"

I heard the refrigerator door slam before Rich answered. "No, I'm a little tired. What I'd like to do is get in a little fishing before we . . . before we . . . you know what I mean."

Lyle sprang out of the chair and dropped the limo key in Barry's lap. "I almost forgot. You've got a date tonight, and I promised you the car. I hope you two have a wonderful evening and talk and talk and talk." He winked at Barry who turned his head in disgust.

"Rich . . ." Lyle shouted upstairs again.

A refrigerator door slammed shut again, only louder this time. "What? I wasn't doing . . . What do you want, Lyle?"

"If you won't go with me tonight, you have to make a list of the supplies we'll need. I searched this whole house, and the only alarm clocks left are digitals. You said they won't work."

Emerging from a bathroom off the foyer Rich said, "Yeah, O.K. It's just little stuff. Should be able to get it at any hardware or department store."

"You could ask Myra if her store sells alarm clocks, Barry," Lyle said while wiggling his eyebrows like Groucho Marx. "No, better not. I don't want anything to be traced to this area."

"Rich . . ." Lyle shouted upstairs again.

"What . . . what?" Rich answered as he re-emerged from the same bathroom.

"If I give Barry the car tonight, and you go fishing, it means I'll have to borrow your truck."

"Yeah, that's all right," Rich answered, almost as if he were relieved.

Lyle looked at me with a touch of sadness in his eyes. "I can't believe I have allowed myself to sink so low," he said.

"Excuse me?" I asked quickly, hoping Lyle had changed his mind.

"I'm going to drive a lousy Toyota. Me, a Cadillac man, in a Toyota truck. That's really low, isn't it? Ah well, a man's got to do what a man's got to do." His mood turned from jocular to serious. "Tonight at 10 we meet back here on the deck to put the final plans together. The timetable has been stepped up. We could be ready to go tomorrow night. Barry, I know you'll be back by 10. Myra has to be at work about that time."

Lyle smirked at both Barry and me, then slowly climbed the winding steps to the upper level, grumbling as he went. "I can't believe myself sometimes. A Toyota. Me in a Toyota truck. I hope nobody sees me." When he reached the top step of the landing, a refrigerator door slammed shut.

Seconds later Rich handed Lyle the keys to the Toyota truck, then headed for another bathroom.

EIGHTEEN

The red light on top of the black-and-white cruiser flip-flopped its beam onto the trees and garage door with an eerie regularity. To me, the dome lights on police cars represent trouble repeating itself over and over again. In this case the symbol became a reality.

I had gone into town for a quiet dinner alone since Lyle had gone to Traverse City, Barry was on his date with Myra, and Rich had taken the ski boat to go fishing. The casual, relaxed, vacation-oriented atmosphere of Suttons Bay was in direct contrast to the tension I was feeling. I had prayed for wisdom and guidance, but I confess to being worried we were on the edge of Hell where prayers might not be heard. Seeing the police cruiser in the yard doubled my anxiety. I stopped along the roadway to guess what had taken place and to collect my thoughts.

My heart was pumping twice as fast as the flashing light on the cruiser. The driver's door of the police car was wide-open. Inside the car, scratchy radio noises sounding like a wood file being drawn across a hard board accelerated my racing pulse.

Rich's truck was parked in the driveway in front of the cruiser. The limousine was not there. It was nine o'clock, and in my agitated state I forgot that Barry might not be back yet. I figured Barry had gone to the police to tell them what we were thinking about doing. That way they could confiscate the plastic explosives and threaten us with jail even if no formal charges could be pressed. In a way I felt relieved just thinking the ordeal might be over. I walked into the house expecting to hear a stern lecture from a couple of rough-looking policemen.

"No formal charges have been brought just yet, you under-stand," I overheard a cop saying as I entered the house. I walked through the foyer to the railing at the edge of the balcony over-looking the lower-level great room. Both the policeman and Lyle looked up at me without saying a word.

"Good evening," I tried to say casually as my voice cracked.

"You'd better come down here," Lyle said flatly. "It looks like we've got trouble."

Instead of two rough-looking policemen, one well-groomed, polite young man who could have passed as a service representa-tive for IBM stood up and shook my hand when I entered the great room. He introduced himself as Officer Timmons. He even apologized for bringing us disturbing news.

"Is there some sort of problem?" I asked, still trying to act casual.

"There could be, although, as I was saying to Mr. Fortrain here, no charges have been filed. Perhaps none will be."

"We can't duck it any longer though," Lyle said quietly. "If we try to pretend a problem doesn't exist, we'd be fooling our-selves."

"That's been my experience too, sir," echoed the polite police-man. He turned to me. "How about you, sir? I understand from Mr. Fortrain you're a man of the cloth. I'm sure you've had to deal with these kinds of things."

"Mmmmhmmm," I nodded, trying to collect my thoughts. "Could I inquire what we're talking about in a little more detail?"

"Sir, forgive me," Office Timmons said humbly. "You didn't hear the first part of this conversation, did you?"

I shook my head and looked at Lyle, who put a finger up to his lips as a signal not to say too much.

"It's Rich," Lyle stated softly.

"Is he under arrest? What's wrong? Where is he?" I blurted out.

"He's all right," said the policeman. "He's sleeping right now."

"In jail? What for?" I asked.

"No sir, he's not in jail. He's here in the house—in one of the bedrooms. He's really all right." The young cop was almost conciliatory.

"He's here, but he's not all right," Lyle corrected.

"Yes, sir. I guess that would be more accurate," the young cop agreed.

Without waiting for any more prompting from me, Lyle explained the whole story. "Seems our boy Rich went fishing tonight. In addition to some fishing tackle and bait, he took a plentiful supply of beer along with him. Apparently the fish weren't biting, so after a while Rich decided to come back home. Except by this time he's in no condition to remember how to get home."

"Uh oh," I groaned.

"Seems he made two or three passes through the marina and . . ."

"Four," corrected Officer Timmons.

"Seems he made four passes through the marina at full speed in the 'No Wake' zone. This got all the boaters upset. Then he buzzed the beach area. This got all the swimmers upset. But his real attention-getter was when he started bearing down on some guy trying to get back to his sailboat in a rubber dinghy."

"Uh oh," I repeated.

"We could look at the positive side of this," the policeman said brightly. "At least there weren't many people out swimming tonight. And no kids got hurt."

"After two or three passes at the guy . . ."

"Three," Officer Timmons agreed.

"After three passes trying to swamp the guy in the rubber dinghy, Rich decided it was time to play Captain Ahab. He pulled alongside the dinghy and tried to harpoon it with his fishing pole."

"You have to understand, no formal charges have been brought just yet," the policeman said to me again. It was as if he was asking me to forgive him for disturbing our evening.

Lyle continued, "Rich's first attempt at capturing the great white dinghy only ended up with a fishing pole in the water. He threw it like a harpoon, but it glanced off the rubber boat and sank into the bay."

"That's innocent enough. Can't press charges for that, can we?" I asked Officer Timmons, who shook his head no.

Lyle also shook his head back and forth, but more in disgust than disagreement. "If that's all our buddy Rich did, we wouldn't have Officer Timmons here, would we?" I had trouble knowing if Lyle was more irritated with Rich or me at that moment. In either case it was clear he was agitated. He continued, "On the next pass Rich decided he would jump off his boat onto the body of the great white dinghy and drive a harpoon straight to the monster's heart."

"Uh oh," I responded.

"You've got a real way with words," Lyle sneered.

"It does get a little complicated," Officer Timmons said in an attempt to cool Lyle down.

Instead of calming down, Lyle started to pace, chewing his nails as he talked. His temper was getting the best of him once again. The smooth, polished salesman had turned into a growling, irritable madman. "So now the jerk jumps onto the dinghy and punches a hole into one side of it. Naturally the guy on board is terrified. So are his wife and kid, who are watching from their sailboat. She calls the Coast Guard, and they send out a helicopter."

"I told you it gets a little complicated," said Officer Timmons. He meant to be helpful, but Lyle became even more agitated. I had to turn my back because I was starting to snicker. I knew this would set Lyle raving.

"The guy in the dinghy takes an oar and tries to knock Rich into the water. He missed. Rich got so mad he struck the other side of the dinghy. Now air is escaping in double time. Meanwhile, Mirkins' ski boat is headed into the marina without a driver."

"Uh oh," I whispered to myself.

"My report says he struck the dinghy two more times, but that's not an important detail," corrected the officer.

Lyle's face was flushed, and he waved his arms as he talked. "What is important is that eventually the guy knocked Rich in the water. This was about fifteen seconds before his dinghy sank beneath him. Meanwhile, the guy's wife is screaming that he doesn't know how to swim."

"He's on a sailboat and a dinghy and he can't swim?" I questioned.

"Happens quite a lot," explained the officer. "I think some people just love the lure of the water and take their chances. It would help if they wore life jackets, but . . ."

"And Rich can't swim either," Lyle said, rolling over the exchange between Timmons and me. "Lucky for both of them, there were boaters in the marina with the presence of mind to get flotation devices to each one."

Officer Timmons joined the explanation by adding, "Preliminary investigations by the Coast Guard showed no need for further helicopter intervention. However, they will be making further inquiries about the suspected use of alcohol and reckless operation of a watercraft."

"Suspected use of alcohol? There were only about seventy people on shore to witness all this," Lyle groaned.

"And what about the ski boat headed toward the marina?" I asked.

"A young man on one of those usually annoying jet skis was able to get into the boat and switch off the ignition before any damage could be done. I'm afraid we'll have to impound the boat as evidence for the evening. If we can meet at the marina tomorrow, I'm sure we can get it back to you." Officer Timmons was continuing to be his helpful, apologetic self.

"This is great, just great," Lyle grumped.

Barry came into the foyer as the three of us were headed up the stairs to escort Officer Timmons to his car. "What's going on?" Barry asked me in a hushed tone as Lyle sat in the car with the officer to fill out a report.

"Great news!" I gushed as I grabbed him by the elbow and

walked him back into the house. "Rich got drunk and almost killed himself and a bunch of other people in the process."

Barry looked at me quizzically. "Ron," he said, "I've been thinking about becoming a Christian for the past three hours. Before I decide, could you explain one more thing to me again?"

"About Jesus and the resurrection?" I asked.

"No. About why you got fired from your last pastorate."

NINETEEN

B arry had been sitting in the lower-level great room since dawn. He was at the piano where he had placed a Bible on the music shelf. As he read the Bible he underlined passages with a hi-liter and made notes in the margins. I didn't notice him as I started up the steps, but at the first landing I caught a glimpse of him out of the corner of my eye. He was so engrossed he didn't even notice me until I cleared my throat dramatically to get his attention. He looked startled at first, but then that wide, toothy grin, cheekbones raised high, with narrow slits for eyes, captured his face.

"Good morning, brother," he said.

I thought I knew what he meant, but I tested it by saying, "You must be reading an interesting score."

He raised the Bible from the shelf and said, "So far it's Jesus 1, the Devil 0. I'm only through the Gospels, but I doubt if it changes."

Excitedly I came down the steps, almost falling as I entered the great room. "You've decided then?" I asked.

"Yes," he said with that same grin. "I don't know what I'm to do next, but I take it from what I've read that the Holy Spirit will do some leading."

"He will! He will!" I exclaimed.

"I'd appreciate your guidance too."

"All I can, I will. You know that. Remember, however, I'm fallible and He is not."

It was hard to tell who was more excited, Barry or I. "I've come up with some ideas," he said. "If there are Christian musical groups, I might be able to help them. Or if youth groups take bicycle tours, I could play a role there. I was training for a triathlon before this trip, so I could help at summer camps with swimming too."

"There are plenty of places for your talents," I laughed. "I envy the pastor who welcomes you into his congregation."

We made our way upstairs to the kitchen, exchanging ideas, patting each other on the back as if we had just won the Super Bowl. Lyle was sitting at the table with a yellow legal-sized tablet in front of him. A white coffee cup with a Cadillac crest on it was next to several colored pencils. The pot of coffee on the kitchen counter was nearly empty. Lyle had been up very early that morning also.

"You guys seem to be in a good mood," Lyle said as he sipped from the Cadillac cup.

"Sharing a few great moments with my brother." I smiled as I clapped Barry on the back.

"That's us . . . brothers for life. I didn't realize you took the fraternity stuff so seriously," Lyle mumbled. "We've got another brother who almost messed up our plans for proving to the world how clever we are."

Barry stepped forward boldly. "Lyle, this joke has gone too far. I've been trying to tell you . . . I'm out of this craziness. Ron's not going to participate either, so let's just drop any further talk about robbing a bank."

Lyle stared at Barry, then back at me. There was such a long silence I could hear the electric clock on the wall whirling its gears as we waited for Lyle's reply.

"Fine," he said. "I thought you two might wimp out on me anyway. So we go to plan B." He sorted through the legal notepapers in front of him and restacked them. The top sheet had a floor plan of the bank, with the vault outlined in red.

"What is plan B?" I asked.

"You and Barry are out of this, Ron. Or don't you remember? Plan B is none of your business."

"Myra is out of this too," Barry warned Lyle.

"Plan B is none of your business either, Barry," Lyle smirked. "You're either with me or against me. There's no middle ground. If you want to tell me what to do and how to do it, you're in. Otherwise, it's none of your business."

Although their comments were icy, Barry and Lyle were raising their voices, nearly shouting at each other. The veins in Barry's neck were bulging as he clenched his teeth and fists.

"Lyle, did anyone ever tell you how obnoxious you are?" Barry shouted.

"I know you're the first one today," Lyle said sarcastically. "However, without a computer I can't give an accurate count across the course of my total life."

"Two more days of freedom and I can't even sleep in because you guys are making such noise," Rich grumbled as he stumbled into the kitchen. The scrambled tufts of hair around his head looked like tiny explosions had taken place within his head. His navel was exposed because the faded blue jeans and sleeveless undershirt he wore stopped several inches from meeting each other. He scratched the gap between the undershirt and the jeans as he opened the refrigerator door.

When Rich stuck his head inside the refrigerator Lyle snarled, "Beer's gone, sunshine."

Rich answered with his head still in the refrigerator, "I know. I was looking for something healthy. Orange juice, or whatever will cure this headache."

Lyle sprang out of his chair and pushed the refrigerator door against Rich's neck, trapping his head within the refrigerator. "You idiot!" he shouted. "I'll give you a headache you'll never cure."

Barry jumped behind Lyle and pulled his arms away from the door while I pulled Rich from behind, prying his head out of the refrigerator compartment. Rich's hair stood straight up around his ears. He could have passed as a vaudeville comedian, especially with the surprised look on his face. "What's a matter with you?" he said with wide-eyed wonderment.

Barry still had a tight grip on Lyle, who shouted even more loudly, "You nearly killed a guy in a lifeboat, you had the whole marina terrorized, and you ask me what's the matter?"

"I don't know what you're talking about," Rich insisted indignantly.

"Yesterday, fool! You do remember yesterday, don't you?" Lyle continued.

I could feel the tension in Rich's body let go, so I released my grip on him, although Barry still clung tightly to Lyle. "I went fishing yesterday," Rich answered absently.

"Then what?" Lyle replied.

"I don't remember," Rich said quietly.

"What do you mean you don't remember?" shouted Lyle as he thrashed in an unsuccessful attempt to break loose from Barry's grip. "What about sinking the dinghy and falling in the water? What about buzzing the marina and the beach? You telling me you don't remember any of that?"

"I don't remember," Rich said absently.

I stood between Rich and Lyle, looking directly into Rich's eyes. "Do you remember going out in the ski boat yesterday?" I asked him.

"Yeah, I did that."

"Did you take any beer with you?" I asked.

"There isn't any beer here. Lyle said so himself," Rich answered.

"That's not the question. Did you take any beer with you?" I repeated.

After a short delay Rich's eyes moistened and he said, "Well, okay, maybe one or two."

"How many?" I asked.

"Five or six," he mumbled.

"How many, Rich?"

"Eight."

"And you drank them all?"

"I hope not."

"You did, you did, you juicehead!" Lyle screamed. "Seventy people watched you. A cop had to bring you here. You can't tell me you don't remember."

"Rich, do you have blackouts?" I asked.

"I suppose."

"Do you?" I insisted.

"So I'm told. I really don't drink that much, you know. I don't think I have a problem. Really. I just don't remember some things."

"Do you remember our little bank plan?" Lyle taunted.

"Yes, I remember, Lyle," said Rich as he arched his back defiantly. "And if you don't stop shouting at me, the whole plan falls apart because I'm the only one who knows how to make the plastic work."

Barry walked Lyle to a chair and pushed him into it. "Rich, Ron and I are out of this thing. Why don't we forget the bank plan. Let's just get you married in a couple of days."

Rich cocked his head to one side, pursed his lips, then scratched his exposed belt line again. "Nah, I don't think so, Barry. See, the bank plan is something I want to do. Getting married is something I don't want to do. I figure I've only got so many breaths left in this life, so I better use them doing what I really want to do."

I tried my hand at it. "Rich, Lyle is just using you."

"Don't listen to him, Rich!" Lyle blurted out.

Rich blinked a few times with a wide-eyed Bambi expression. He looked directly at me and said, "Of course he's using me. But I'm using him right back. Ron, from the time we were in college together I knew Lyle was going to do something big. I also knew I didn't have much self-confidence, or brains, or courage, or whatever it takes to do anything except show up for work in the morning and go home at night. My biggest ambition was to hook on with a really big company and hope nobody found out I couldn't do much until I retired. For a while I had it wired. After the service I hired on with a big engineering outfit but couldn't survive a headcount reduction when the first recession hit. They said it was economics, but I knew better. They could see I didn't have the talent. They used the recession as an excuse."

"But Rich, a bank . . ." I protested.

He interrupted me with, "I hate banks Ron. I took a loan to start my own business. They knew I didn't have the talent to stay with it. They just wanted to confiscate everything I owned. Lyle has put it all together for me. I get even with banks and at the same time I get to prove to myself that I do have some courage, self-confidence, and brains. Lyle knows it can't happen without my knowledge of the plastic. That shows I do have brains. I just need somebody to supply me with some of the other stuff—the self-confidence and guts to go through with it. Lyle has those things, Ron. So, sure he's using me. We're using each other."

Barry loosened his grip on Lyle, who was sitting smugly at the table with a closed-mouth grin on his face. Wrapping a muscular arm around Rich, Barry said gently, "But, Rich, it doesn't have to be this way. There are so many ways you could . . ."

Rich interrupted him. "Barry, that's easy for you to say. You've got more talent than Disney World. I'm just a Little Leaguer who only got in the game when the home team was ahead by ninety-six runs. Lyle's giving me a chance at going in the game when it really matters."

Rich turned away from Barry and me. He reopened the refrigerator, looking over his shoulder once to make sure Lyle didn't attack from the rear again. But Lyle had no intention of attacking his only ally. Instead, he said in a triumphant way, "Besides, we're brothers. Right, Rich?"

Rich turned around with a plastic carton of orange juice in his hand, holding it up as if he were making a toast. "Brothers. Brothers for life."

Lyle held up a coffee cup, returning the toast. "To brothers! Long may they live!"

TWENTY

The only agreements we reached were that we should retrieve Mirkin's ski boat at the marina and try to make amends to the people on the sailboat, including the replacement of their punctured dinghy. Rich had the entire incident explained to him by Lyle, whose mood had turned from angry to amused. Lyle volunteered to pay for the cost of the dinghy under two conditions. First, Rich had to apologize to the family on the sailboat; next, he had to give up drinking until after his wedding. Lyle never mentioned the bank plan. He had no need to speak about it since Rich was clearly in support of doing whatever Lyle suggested.

Barry and I did not have time to discuss what we would do, but I was now regretting that I hadn't taken Barry's suggestion of leaving a couple of days earlier. It appeared this was the wiser path to follow since Lyle and Rich could not be persuaded to abandon the insanity which had grown from a moment of weakness. What was repulsive to Barry and me was attractive to Lyle and Rich. What we considered immoral, they considered a challenge.

But Barry couldn't leave either, because of the guilt he felt about accidentally involving Myra in Lyle's scheme. And I did not want to go until I was sure I had exhausted every possibility of derailing this train of sin which seemed to be gaining steam with each passing moment. The idea of calling on the police to intervene was not what I wanted to do, but it was fast becoming a necessity under the circumstances. Losing the friendship of Lyle and Rich was not a negative consequence to me compared to the alternatives.

As we rode to the marina in Lyle's limousine, the irony of it all struck me: the same event drawing us together to rekindle past friendships would split us apart forever. I remember missing my wife at that moment more than I had ever missed her before. Where the feeling had come from, I still don't know. I had not thought of her too often since the trip began; I hadn't even called to let her know I had arrived safely. I made a mental note to call her in the evening when I knew she would be home from work.

We pulled into the parking lot of the marina and headed for the harbormaster's station. The harbormaster was a slight, blond man with a full beard that seemed to grow up from his open-necked white starched shirt. JIM was stenciled in red script letters above his breast pocket. Jim's hair was pulled back into a ponytail held in place with a green rubber band. He wore a white painter's cap that looked like it had been worn during the painting of a number of barns since it was splattered with confetti-like splashes of red and white.

"Jim," said Lyle with great charm and a wide smile, "I'm Lyle Fortrain. I'm here with my friends to see if we can recover a ski boat belonging to Mr. Mirkin. You might know it . . . it's an eighteen-footer."

"Yeah, I know it," answered Jim with a twinkle in his eye. Like Officer Timmons, he sounded apologetic for holding the boat. "Sure, you can take it any time. I'll have to charge you for one night's mooring, however. Sorry . . . it's the rules of the village council."

"That's it?" asked Lyle. "The police don't want to impound it or anything?"

"Can't," Jim answered with a smile. "People on the sailboat didn't press any charges. In fact, they left this morning before sunrise. I think they were afraid something else might happen. Say, you weren't the driver of the ski boat, were you?"

Rich stood sheepishly behind Lyle, hoping not to be noticed.

"No. Why do you ask?" Lyle said.

"Well, I wasn't on duty when the incident took place, but I'll bet I've heard the story twenty times today. It's a lucky thing nobody was hurt, especially the ski boat driver."

"Couldn't he swim?" asked Lyle innocently.

"Oh, I don't know about that," Jim answered. "But see the big ketch out there—the forty-footer anchored out a ways? The skipper of that boat had a gun trained on the ski boat driver. He told me this morning he was about to pull the trigger, but he was afraid of hitting the guy who owned the dinghy."

"Do you think he was serious, or was he just talking?" Lyle asked.

Jim had a twinkle in his eye, suggesting he believed it was real. "Can't say for sure," he answered. "Some folks are all talk, but you get an idea others are for real. I don't think he's much for making things up. He said his silver Mercedes would be delivered here this morning, and that's it pulling in the yard." Jim pointed to a shiny silver Mercedes with blacked-out windows.

Lyle looked stunned. He stared at the car, then out to the ketch, and back to the car again. "What's the name of that boat?" he asked Jim in a demanding tone.

"Gee, I don't remember offhand. We can check the register . . ."

"Is it *The Circuit Breaker*?" Lyle asked quickly.

"Yeah, I think it is . . . Out of Chicago."

"What's the captain's name? The one with the Mercedes."

"It's on the register too. It was like a movie star's . . ."

"Granger," Lyle said as a statement, not a question.

"I think that's it."

"Where is he? I've got to see him."

"He hasn't been here since last night. He was dressed like he was going to meet someone. Haven't seen him since," Jim answered politely.

"Get to the car!" Lyle commanded the three of us with a swoop of his arm.

Rich followed him immediately, while Barry and I stood there as confused as poor Jim, who shouted at Lyle, "Hey, Mr. Fortrain, what do you want me to do with the ski boat?"

"Sink it, sell it, give it away . . . I could care less," Lyle shouted over his shoulder as he began to sprint to the white Cadillac limousine.

PART III

TWENTY-ONE

Rich was three steps behind Lyle and slid into the front passenger seat. Barry and I walked slowly to the limousine, looking at each other with a shrug of the shoulders and a vague notion that Lyle's agitation was once again connected to a silver Mercedes. Unlike the Mercedes we chased after leaving the restaurant, this car was larger and appeared as if it had just been washed and polished. I know little about automobiles, especially expensive ones, but I was sure this was not the same car we had seen earlier.

Beads of sweat were running down the back of Lyle's neck. His hands were clenched around the steering wheel so tightly, his knuckles turned white. Barry was sitting behind Rich, who looked at us with a wide-eyed expression which said he didn't know what was going on. Barry patted Rich on the arm a couple of times to reassure him everything would be all right.

"It's him. It's really him!" Lyle hissed through clenched teeth.

"It's all my fault, isn't it?" Rich asked no one of us in particular. "I did something really bad to cause this, didn't I?"

"This is something different, I think," Barry said to Rich.

"Did I do something else besides what you told me?" Rich asked Lyle.

"He's here. It's almost too good to be true," Lyle said with an eagerness in his voice.

"Did I do something good?" Rich asked expectantly.

"We've got to find him, follow him. I want to talk to him face to face. Tonight, tomorrow, whatever it takes. He'll be around."

"Lyle, I'm not following this. How long was I blacked out?" asked Rich with a puzzled expression on his face.

"I'll explain it to you later, Rich," Lyle answered tersely. "We've got some important things to get done before your wedding."

"Right," said Rich with a grin. "Did you get some alarm clocks like I told you? How about the thin copper wire?"

"I got it all, but the bank scheme is off," Lyle stated bluntly.

Barry and I looked at each other as if we were checking to see if we had heard correctly. I leaned back in the seat with a sigh of relief. Barry smiled and shook his head as if he were clearing it.

"What do you mean it's off?" Rich protested.

"There's a more important task to get done. There's something I've got to do . . ."

"What about us? What about me?" Rich whined.

"I'll need you guys to help me. In fact, I probably can't do this without your help," Lyle answered. "Besides, what I would like to do isn't illegal, so we won't get in trouble like the bank idea. Ron and Barry were going to pull out if we went ahead with the bank job anyway."

"So what?" Rich asked in a loud, demanding voice. "We knew that was going to happen. We talked about it yesterday morning."

Lyle's face was flushed as he looked at Barry and me. "He's confused," he said. "The booze must have done something to his memory."

"It's all right." I smiled, knowing Lyle was lying again.

"But I want to know what this brainstorm is before I agree to anything," Barry interjected.

"Why?" Rich protested. "Why are we giving up on the bank? Just because you changed your mind, Lyle? Who made you king?"

"Shut up!" Lyle shouted at Rich.

"I don't have to shut up," Rich answered with the pout of a five-year-old. "What about showing the world we can do whatever we put our minds to? What about all that talk of achieving anything we wanted if we didn't get shafted by the system?"

"If you must know the truth, I never intended to go through with the bank idea anyway. It was just something to . . ."

"That's a lie!" Rich snarled.

"It's not," Lyle protested. "Rich, why would I be part of robbing a bank if I didn't plan to keep the money?"

"What did I care if you didn't want the money?" Rich replied. "I was going to keep it if you wanted to be that dumb."

Lyle grabbed Rich by the shirt collar. "Why you little, lyin' . . ."

"Cut it out, both of you," I said as I grabbed Lyle and Barry pulled at Rich.

"You're rotten!" Rich said to Lyle as tears welled in his eyes. "You lie all the time. You've always been a liar. You let me believe in something, then you took it away."

"You let yourself believe in things, not me. You choose to believe whatever you like. I can't make you believe anything."

"Don't give me that dime-store-psychology baloney. You're a terrible person. You've always been a terrible person, and I don't care whether you choose to believe that or not."

"If I'm so terrible, why did you keep sending me all those letters about what we were doing since college? Why didn't you just knock me off the mailing list?" Lyle asked angrily.

Rich didn't answer right away. He leaned back against the door of the limousine, closed his eyes, and exhaled a long sigh through his nose. When he opened his eyes he said, "Believe it or not, it's because you three are the closest I've ever been to anyone in my life. Even worse, Lyle, you're the best friend I've ever had. Twenty years after graduation, and you three are the best I can do. Boy, there's proof of a wasted life."

The tears were still in his eyes as Lyle, Barry, and I exchanged quick glances with each other to avoid eye contact with Rich. Perhaps it was the relief of knowing the bank job was off, perhaps it was Rich's remarks, maybe it was the whimsical look in Barry's eyes, or the stunned expression on Lyle's face, but whatever it was, I somehow imagined myself looking down on the four of us in the

white Cadillac limousine and I began to snicker. The next to laugh
was Rich; he punched Lyle on the shoulder good-naturedly. In the
minutes that followed, we laughed, we gave each other the secret
fraternity handshake, we sang the fraternity sweetheart song, we
sang the fraternity fight song, and if there had been an American
flag in the car, we probably would have sung the "National
Anthem."

"To brothers!" Lyle exclaimed as he stuck his right hand forward.

"To brothers!" we answered as we piled our right hands on top
of his.

"Brothers for life!" we shouted in unison.

The driver of the Mercedes was a female college student from
Leland. She had been hired by "a Mr. Granger" to drive his car
to Suttons Bay so he could have ground transportation when he
arrived. She had planned to meet him when he anchored, but
instead of stopping overnight in Northport as he indicated at first,
Mr. Granger went straight to Suttons Bay. Jim, the harbormaster,
said he knew of three or four couples each year who charted sailing trips around the Great Lakes and had their cars ferried from
port to port as Mr. Granger was doing. Rental cars were scarce,
even unavailable, in the smaller villages of Michigan and
Wisconsin.

Lyle questioned the young woman about Granger's physical
description, complexion, and dress. When she seemed reluctant to
disclose much information about someone who had given her fifty
dollars just to wash a car and drive it fifteen miles, Lyle told her
Granger was a college classmate of ours whom we planned to
meet in Suttons Bay. Thinking this was true, the young woman
volunteered all she could about Mr. Granger, including a detailed
account of his jewelry. Somehow his jewelry seemed to stand out
in her mind even more than his height or weight, which she
summed up as "about average." She remembered he wore three
gold chains of varying lengths around his neck; one was a thick

rope chain in the center of two thinner ones. On his right hand was a gold nugget ring with three diamonds, while his left hand was adorned with a cat's-eye pinky ring.

Lyle tried to pry out more details about Granger's looks, but the young woman said he was "kind of old, probably in his forties," then looked at the three of us, blushed, and said she had to go. When Lyle asked if she knew Mr. Granger's first name she said, "Sure. It's Donald, same as my boyfriend's," then she walked away from the marina parking lot.

Donald Granger was the second husband of Lyle's ex-wife. Donald Granger was also the only person who really knew how Louise Fortrain had died two years ago, and now he was in Leelanau County, Michigan. More accurately, Donald Granger's boat and car were in Leelanau County, Michigan, but his whereabouts were unknown.

Lyle was visibly shaken. He paced, mumbled things to himself, and threw out one idea after another about finding Donald Granger. Rich, Barry, and I said very little to Lyle until he stopped himself, admitting again he needed our help. This time, instead of creating a plan we would be expected to follow, Lyle asked for our input, suggestions and ideas. The final objective was a face to face confrontation between Lyle and Granger about Louise's death so Lyle would not have to live the rest of his life wondering how she died.

When we asked about the police department's account of her death, Lyle scoffed at the incomplete nature of their investigation, stating they dismissed it as an accident with little or no investigation. It was a case of two people aboard a boat, with no way to refute Donald Granger's version of the story without any evidence of foul play. Lyle only had three chances to talk with Granger about Louise's death. Each time Granger arranged to have employees or family members present. Calls to Granger were never answered or returned. Still haunting Lyle was the conversation two week's prior to Louise's death when she wondered out loud what business her husband was conducting beyond electrical contracting. Lyle wanted only one hour with Granger; an hour where he could watch Granger's eyes, listen to Granger's voice, pick up movements in Granger's body language that would tell him the true story behind Louise's death. Although Louise was gone, Lyle had never let go. He would never be able to do so until he knew without a doubt what had caused her to die so mysteriously on a summer's evening two years ago while sailing on *The Circuit Breaker*.

"Here I was looking to show the world I could achieve something meaningful in my life, and Granger shows up. This is exactly what I've been looking for. Getting to the bottom of, or at least gaining a lead on, the real cause of Louise's death may be the biggest accomplishment of my life. But I can't do it without you three. I'm sorry about the bank idea. It was something to keep us occupied while we were together. This is for real though. What can I do? How can we find him? What should I say?" Lyle asked painfully.

Barry said Granger obviously had to return to his boat or his car before too long. While the harbormaster had Granger registered for a five-day stay, it was Barry's guess that Granger would return to the boat to sleep, or would pick up the car to drive to a motel in the area. We all agreed Granger would come to us in time, even if we couldn't find him.

Time, however, was what we no longer had in plentiful supply since Rich's wedding was only two days away. Rich volunteered to postpone the wedding until after we found Granger. Lyle dismissed his suggestion before Barry or I could say a word.

I suggested that we split up and meet back at the marina every two hours to compare notes. Barry said he would alert Myra in case Granger bought anything at the department store. I would revisit the barber shop. Rich volunteered to stop at the local bars and restaurants, but we diverted him to the motels in the area. Lyle would drive the limousine to various tourist spots hoping to spot Granger. Rich, Barry, and I were only to follow Granger if we found him. We were not to talk to him, but we could alert Lyle by calling the car phone in the limousine. While we hadn't settled on the best method to confront Granger, we agreed the four of us

BROTHERS FOR LIFE 139

should stay together in case he was armed. From that point Lyle could question Granger so the truth could be learned.

Lyle seemed genuinely touched by our willingness to help. He choked back tears as he shook hands with Barry and me. He grabbed Rich behind the back of the neck with his left hand and pulled Rich's face to his own. "Do you forgive me?" he asked.

"Sure. We're brothers, aren't we?" Rich answered softly.

Lyle put a hand on each of Rich's shoulders, looked him squarely in the eyes, and said, "Brothers. Brothers for life."

There was a long silence in the car. We sat absolutely still. I remember feeling a surge of adrenaline then—I was bursting to begin the hunt for the mysterious Donald Granger who had silently slipped into our lives and was about to change them forever.

TWENTY-TWO

During the next eight hours Donald Granger managed to elude the four of us to the point where I was beginning to wonder if he knew we were trying to find him and he was hiding from us out of spite. We met every two hours as planned, but not a single clue turned up regarding Granger's whereabouts. There were no car rental agencies in Suttons Bay, and he had not returned for his Mercedes. We surmised he was on foot or had been met by someone who was driving. It seemed there was little hope we would find him before the wedding. The thought of staying for the full five days Granger was registered with the harbormaster crossed my mind, but I was hoping to get home immediately after Rich's ceremony. Barry had other commitments that would take him back to his teaching duties. This meant Lyle would be left alone, unless Rich could convince his bride to spend a honeymoon in the back of a Toyota pickup truck.

Even though Granger had been able to elude us, I knew the only way he could escape the summer heat was to be inside an air-conditioned building. The afternoon temperature soared into the nineties. Waves of heat bounced off the sidewalks. Imaginary puddles of water in the street let me believe it was cooler than it felt. The puddles would disappear in a quick, cruel vanishing act to remind me they were only illusions while the heat was reality. The frozen custard and ice cream stands were packed with lines of irritable parents trying to control equally irritable children who pinched, punched, and pulled at each other's sweaty bodies with dirty hands made grimy by layers of perspiration and sand. Near the end of the afternoon I visited an air-conditioned art gallery for an hour just to be out of the heat. I looked at every painting, photograph, and piece of jewelry in the store at least three times. I guiltily bought a small aerial photograph of a cherry orchard to keep the store owner from thinking I was a vagrant. I had no use for the picture except as a gift, but the price was worth the hour of air-conditioned comfort I spent in the gallery.

When I felt I had overstayed my welcome in the gallery, even with the purchase of the guilt-framed photograph, I slowly made my way back to the park. The park itself was a grass- and tree-covered rectangle adjacent to the beach, directly north of the marina.

In the center of the park, sitting on a bench beneath an oak shade tree, was Barry Gieselmann, seemingly undisturbed by the heat or anything else in life. He was wearing a pair of red floral swimming shorts and a yellow T-shirt, his bare feet buried in the sand. Beneath the park bench were his jogging shoes with laces sloppily untied, looking more wilted than he. His hair was wet and slicked back; I determined he had been swimming. He slowly raised and lowered a small brown book in front of his face like some form of mystic exercise. His left arm was draped casually over the back of the park bench. I resented his relaxed appearance as much as I hated the sheets of warm air wrapped around me as I marched toward the park bench.

"What are you doing?" I asked him angrily.

"Memorizing Scripture. It's the Christian thing to do on a day like this," he said in a cool, unbothered voice as he lifted a pocket-sized New Testament for me to see. "'For all have sinned and fall short of the glory of God.' Romans 3, verse 23."

"That's very nice," I said with no enthusiasm. I was hoping it would pass him by, but it didn't.

"'And he said to them, "O foolish men and slow of heart to believe in all that the prophets have spoken! Was it not necessary for the Christ to suffer these things and to enter into His glory?"' Do you know where that's from?" Barry asked, then answered without a chance for me to respond, "It's Luke 24, verses 25 and 26."

"We're supposed to be finding Granger for Lyle, and our time is running out," I replied defensively.

"'But seek first His kingdom, and His righteousness; and all these things shall be added to you.' It's Matthew 6 something, I think. Let me see. Yep, it's 6:33."

I was too tired, hungry, hot, and irritable not to let it show. "While we were out running around the county trying to find Granger, you've been swimming and memorizing Scriptures?"

Barry answered, "'And we know that God causes all things to work together for good to those who love God, to those who are called according to His purpose.' Romans 8, verse 28. I like that one."

I was getting furious. I didn't know if he was mocking me, but his cavalier attitude mixed with the heat caused me to erupt. "I was out beating the bushes for this guy and you're laying here taking life easy? Learning the Scriptures is all right, but . . ."

"'Greater love has no one than this, that one lay down his life for his friends.' I don't remember where that one comes from," he said while scratching his head.

"The book of John!" I exploded.

"I know that much."

"John 15 something," I said a little less sternly.

He thumbed through his little Testament quickly. I could see he had underlined and dog-eared it for quick reference. "You got it! It's John 15:13. I hope someday I can be as skilled as you regarding the Bible," he said with sincerity.

His remark brought me to a sudden halt. In being so caught up in the chase of a person I didn't even know, I was not only neglecting Barry's spiritual growth but my own as well. "I'm sorry I yelled at you. I've been . . ."

"Verily, verily, I say unto you, Granger is on his boat even as we speaketh. That would be a King James version, I believe." Barry winked.

"What did you say?" I shot back.

"It would be a King James version. They seem to have a lot of verily, verilies and speaketh in that edition . . ."

"Not that part, fool!" I laughed. "The first part."

"Granger is on his boat. It's true, but it's not very Scriptural."

"When did you . . . How did you . . . When did he . . . "

"Did people have trouble following your sermons, Ron, or is it just me?"

"Come on, come on, come on!" I said as I waved my hands for him to tell me the whole situation.

He needed no additional prompting. "I was getting real hot out here, so I thought I'd stop by the store to see Myra and buy some cooler clothes. I bought these shorts and shirt on sale. What do you think?"

"They look awful," I groaned.

"I know Christians aren't supposed to lie, but couldn't you be a little more subtle?"

"I'm dying of curiosity and you want me to talk about red, floral underwear?" I answered impatiently.

"Not underwear. Swimming trunks."

"They're really you," I said. "Now are you happy?"

He bowed at the waist, then indicated a spot for me to sit next to him on the bench. He looked over both shoulders to make sure no one would hear. He said in a very low voice, "Actually I ran across him by mistake. I was goofing off in the department store, trying to impress Myra, when this guy with two big bags of groceries came out of the store across the street. At first I didn't think anything of it, but when he wasn't headed for a car and looked like he might go to the marina, I started to follow him. He was having a terrible time with the groceries because the bags were so heavy. He also had been drinking most of the afternoon."

"How do you know?" I asked.

"He told me."

"You talked to him?"

"I offered to help him with his groceries. It's the Christian thing to do, isn't it?"

My excitement couldn't be contained. "So what did he say?"

"Said he had been drinking all afternoon."

"Other stuff. Are you sure it was him?"

Barry shrugged his shoulders. "At first I didn't know for sure. He fit the college kid's description though. He looked 'about average' and wore all the trinkets she said he had. As we walked through the parking lot, he pointed to the silver Mercedes and said he should have driven it to the store but didn't think he should be drinking and driving. A very concerned citizen, this Donald Granger. He bought the groceries for a trip to Charlevoix. Do you know where that is?"

I shook my head no.

"Anyway, we walked right down to a dinghy and loaded the groceries in it. He offered me a drink aboard *The Circuit Breaker*—even wanted to pay me for helping him. He talked plenty before he shoved off. Said he was from Chicago, taking a month to sail around Lake Michigan. Said he always anchors out, never ties up at a port even though it would be more convenient. He said he likes the isolation. Gets enough of people the other eleven months of the year. He sails that big ketch alone."

I was puzzled. "What do you make of it?"

"Can't say for sure. Granger really didn't seem so bad," Barry confessed. "In some ways he's a lot easier to take than Lyle. Still, there is something about him that didn't ring true. I can't describe it exactly. Maybe he's a wolf in sheep's clothing. There must be a Bible verse to fit this situation."

"Something unusual is happening. I can't put my finger on it either. There is a verse in Matthew we need to pay attention to, my friend. It goes, 'Behold, I send you out as sheep in the midst of wolves; therefore be shrewd as serpents, and innocent as doves.' Something says that's what God is telling us right now."

Suddenly, from behind me, I heard two sharp banging noises like a gun being fired rapidly.

TWENTY-THREE

Barry leaned to one side momentarily. His head slumped over, then his neck angd shoulders struck my lap before he rolled off the bench and fell onto the ground in front of me. I spun around expecting to see a gunman off in the distance.

Instead, Rich and Lyle were standing in an elevated parking area by the white Cadillac limousine. Lyle was carrying an over-sized bucket of fried chicken, while Rich toted two six-packs of soda pop.

"What's the matter with Barry?" Rich shouted as he ran down a short incline toward us. "Did he faint from the heat?"

I looked back and forth from Barry to Rich three times. "I don't know," I said. "I thought he was shot."

I looked at Barry again. He opened his eyes. A wide toothy grin swallowed his face as the eyes disappeared into their familiar slits. "You jerk!" I said, trying to sound mad but too relieved to be convincing.

Lyle walked down a grassy knoll toward the bench, where he placed the bucket of freshly fried chicken. "He does that a lot," Lyle said in disgust. "He was poisoned at the airport, now he's shot in the park."

"You were poisoned at the airport?" Rich asked incredulously.

"Yeah, by an angry Chinaman," Barry said as he brushed himself off.

"Korean," I corrected as I pushed him on the shoulder.

"Whatever. They all look alike," was his answer.

"Nice to see you two having such a good time," Lyle broke in. "I suspect you've been yukking it up while Rich and I were trying to find Granger. Looks like you've been swimming, Barry."

"Did you bring us something to eat?" asked Barry as he rubbed his hands together. "I'm starved."

"Thought you might be," Rich said as he popped open a couple of cold sodas. "I wasn't allowed to bring beer," he grumbled.

Barry replied, "This is better for you anyway. I'll bet you were on your best behavior and didn't even go inside a bar today."

Rich puffed out his chest. "That's right. I promised, and I kept my word. It was like an oath."

I said, "I thought I heard gun shots."

"It was the slamming of the Toyota and limo doors. What's got you so jumpy?" Lyle asked as he tore the lid off the bucket of chicken.

Barry put his hand on my arm before I could answer. "I saw you guys parking on the upper level out of the corner of my eye. Before we eat, I'd like to ask the blessing for our food."

"Say what?" asked Lyle. "Don't tell me you've become one of those holy rollers like Ron."

"Shall we bow our heads?" Barry continued.

"It's only a lousy bucket of fried chicken," protested Lyle.

Barry began, "Heavenly Father . . ."

"We're in the middle of a park, for cryin' out loud . . ."

"Heavenly Father," Barry repeated in a louder voice. I don't know if Lyle bowed his head or not. At least he kept quiet through the prayer.

"Thank you, that was very nice," I said to Barry when he finished.

"It was nice," added Rich. "We used to pray at our meals when I was a kid. I wonder why I got away from it?"

Lyle ripped the meat off a drumstick with his front teeth. "I'm trying to track my wife's killer, and we're talking about praying over a bucket of chicken."

For the next twenty minutes we listened to Rich and Lyle vent frustrations about their inability to find any clue of Granger. Lyle had been to the gambling casino at the Indian reservation in Peshabestown, to Fish Town in Leland, to the golf course at Sugar Loaf, the sand dunes at Sleeping Bear National Park, the Grout estate on Bass Lake, and all the way south to Traverse City. Rich covered all the motels in the immediate area, then went south to Traverse City along the "strip" where motels seemed to outnumber visitors, yet were always fully occupied.

No motel operator had seen Granger. One even passed along discouraging news that there were many new bed-and-breakfast establishments springing up in the area, so Granger could be holed up in someone's house without much difficulty.

I was almost exploding with eagerness to tell Lyle and Rich that Barry and I knew exactly where Granger was. However, I could see Barry wanted to continue to keep it quiet, for reasons I didn't understand. He kept stuffing himself with fried chicken, casually licking his fingers as the other two told of one fruitless attempt after another to locate Granger. When he finally spoke, Barry changed the subject so radically I was totally mystified by what he was doing.

"Say, Lyle," he began, "remember when we were in college and I was dating that French girl with the beautiful long hair?"

Lyle wrinkled his nose and forehead as if he didn't know what brought up such a subject. Truthfully, I didn't know what direction Barry was taking either. After almost too quick a pause, Lyle answered, "I don't know what you're talking about Gieselmann. What's this got to do with finding Granger?"

"Remember that night in the parlor of the house? You came in late from a date and I was playing the piano?"

"Gieselmann, you were always playing the piano. How am I supposed to remember something over twenty years ago?"

"And we talked for a long time that night. Even stayed up until dawn and went to breakfast together."

"Does this have *anything* to do with Granger?" Lyle asked impatiently.

"I told you that night I was really crazy about the French girl. Her name was Monique. You must remember her, with a name like that. I went so far as to say she was the woman I was going to marry someday."

Lyle picked up the pop bottles and napkins we had used. He stuffed them into a paper sack, never looking directly at Barry. "I don't know what you're talking about, Gieselmann, but I've got more important things on my mind than reminiscing about our post-puberty memories."

"The next week you asked Monique out. You started dating her. I was so mad at you I couldn't see straight. But instead of talking to *you* about it, I stopped talking to her. You keep telling me how smart I am. Does that sound smart to you? I never said another word to her . . . I just let her go." Barry rose from the park bench, his large leg muscles bulging as he stood. Barry's physical power through years of bicycling was evident and imposing. He slowly walked toward Lyle.

"What are you talking about, Gieselmann? You're a nut case! I think you've been in the sun too long!" chanted Lyle, his voice rising with each sentence.

I was ready to spring at Barry, although I didn't welcome the opportunity. I looked at Rich hoping he would help, but he was in such a state of wide-eyed amazement I couldn't tell what he might do.

Barry clapped a hand on Lyle's shoulder, holding him steady. "I just want you to know I forgive you, and I hope you will forgive me too," Barry said directly.

"What's going on here? Where is this coming from?" asked a stunned Lyle.

"'For if you forgive men for their transgressions, your heavenly Father will also forgive you. But if you do not forgive men, then your Father will not forgive your transgressions.' It's from Matthew 6, verses 14 and 15."

Lyle didn't say anything at first. Barry took his hand away from Lyle's shoulder, then picked up the litter around the bench, stuffing it in the paper sack Lyle was holding. Lyle stood with his mouth open as Barry stuffed the empty bucket of chicken into the sack.

"All right. O.K., Gieselmann, you want to know why I did it?" blurted Lyle.

"No. It's not important."

"You want to know why, don't you? That's why you did that forgiveness routine."

"It's just something I had to do," Barry replied.

"I'll tell you if you want me to tell you. You're going to force me into it, aren't you?" Lyle was shaking. His temper was getting hold of him, taking him to places he might later regret.

"Lyle, I forgive you. That's all you need to know. All I need to know is that you forgive me also." Barry was so calm, in direct contrast to Lyle.

"I'm not going to forgive you! I'm going to tell you why I . . ."

Barry held up one hand, like a policeman halting traffic. "Lyle, there's one more thing you should know."

"What? What now? You going to give me another Bible verse?"

"Ron and I know where Granger is," Barry stated quietly.

Lyle said nothing. He staggered on wobbly legs to the park bench. He sat down like a prizefighter who had been hit in the head with a strong right cross, eyes glazed, mouth open, not sure of himself or his surroundings, yet still having enough sense to know there were some important rounds to go before the finish.

TWENTY-FOUR

Night did not fall on Suttons Bay that evening. Rather, it came by some mysteriously slow movement which seemed to keep the sun suspended forever. With the sun at our backs and *The Circuit Breaker* anchored at the marina in front of us, we had a clear view of Granger in the event he decided to come ashore.

Lyle thanked Barry and patted him on the back so many times I thought Barry would develop welts. Now that Granger had been delivered to Lyle, a new puzzle surfaced—how to talk to Granger. Based on Barry's conversation with him, we concluded Granger would stay aboard *The Circuit Breaker* all night. His Mercedes was parked and locked. At the same time, its mere presence indicated Granger did not intend to spend his remaining four days in Suttons Bay aboard a boat. We were unable to leave the area in case Granger left the boat. At the same time, we did not have the luxury of four days to wait for him since Rich's fiancée was due to arrive the next afternoon.

The plan we developed was more courageous than smart, and even more foolhardy than courageous. We agreed that if Granger did not come to us by nightfall, we would go to him. What we lacked was a way to get to a boat anchored hundreds of feet from shore in twenty-five feet of water.

"No problem," Lyle said as he walked away from us to the harbormaster's office. "You found Granger—I'll find a way to get us to him."

Within a half hour the harbormaster provided us with a rubber raft abandoned at the marina two years earlier. An oversized black and yellow Zodiac, the raft was hidden in a storage area where it had been purged of its air but allowed to collect all the dust it could hold. We washed it in the water by the boat launch ramp, then loaded it into the bed of Rich's pickup truck. The raft was so big, it looked like a black and yellow dirigible had landed in the back of the truck.

"It's a beauty," Rich grunted as we helped him unload the raft.

"Big enough for all four of us," Lyle said with a nod.

"Why would anyone leave this?" I asked Jim, who was curious about our use of the raft.

"Beats me," he shrugged. "A bunch of yuppie types in BMWs had it here two years ago for a beach party. They left a note on it saying the raft had now joined the legions of the homeless. Said to chalk it up to the policies of the Reagan Administration. Do any of you understand what that means?" he asked. "What did Reagan's policies have to do with rubber rafts?"

"Not much," Barry agreed.

"I mean, this thing is worth three, maybe four hundred dollars. Say, are you the scuba diver?" Jim asked Barry.

"The what?"

"Mr. Fortrain said one of you was a dive master and you needed the raft for a night dive. I know there are plenty of shiny fishing lures at the bottom of the bay, but I don't think I ever heard a story about a barge with bars of silver sinking out there."

"Is that what he said?" Barry asked. "Anything else?"

"Said he might clue me in about where it could be if you don't find it tonight. I've never been scuba diving, but I could learn if what he says about those bars of silver is right."

"Sometimes Mr. Fortrain talks too much," I told Jim.

He winked at me. "Gotcha! The secret is safe with me."

I tried to talk to Lyle about the story he had given Jim, but he laughed it off with an insincere apology. I could see I would get nowhere with Lyle. His energy level had risen to a feverish pitch.

I knew a sermon about failing to tell the truth would be ignored regardless of accuracy or delivery technique.

"Let's review it again," Lyle said like a football coach, clapping his hands, pacing as he talked, making sure nothing was missing from the game plan. "Once it gets dark we paddle the Zodiac out to *The Circuit Breaker* as quietly as we possibly can. I'm up the boarding ladder first, then Barry, then Ron. Rich, you stay in the raft in case there's trouble. The three of us have to be on our toes because he has a gun."

"I don't think he has a gun. I'm sure he was just trying to sound tough to Jim," I interjected hopefully.

"Ron, we are not planning a Sunday school picnic. From this moment on we are dealing with evil, moral corruption, and sin. And we are not dealing with it in the abstract, like some sermon from a safe pulpit. We are about to come against it face to face. Granger will have a gun, believe me." Lyle was more than direct with me. He came across as condescending, and I resented his pompous approach in front of the others.

"When do you want me to come aboard?" Rich asked.

"After we're sure Granger won't try any funny stuff. Ron or Barry can give you a signal. Just make sure you have the Zodiac secured to *The Circuit Breaker*."

Rich nodded. "I won't forget. I don't know how to swim. The raft is my salvation."

"What's the purpose of this visit?" Barry asked Lyle.

"I just want one hour with him down below. No rough stuff, just some hardball questions the cops never asked. In fact, you can keep the time for me, Gieselmann. Let me know when the hour is up so he can't go hollering to the cops about breaking and entering or some Mickey Mouse law."

Barry persisted, "Are you sure we aren't breaking some law?"

Lyle was becoming impatient. "We're just visiting an old acquaintance of mine. He even invited you to join him earlier."

"No rough stuff, right?" Barry continued.

"Gieselmann, have I ever lied to you?"

Barry simply stared at Lyle.

"Within the last hour, I mean."

Barry continued to stare.

"O.K., O.K., no rough stuff. You have my word."

We reviewed the plan at least three more times before the sun set. I had hoped for darkness to overtake us quickly. My nerves were becoming more frayed the longer we delayed, but the sun became a temperamental child, rebelling against going to bed until it was ready to do so. The bloody red-orange light flooding the west eventually gave way to a black silk sky dotted by a tiara of rhinestone stars. We let another hour pass so the blackness of the night could swallow any trace of sun that might have existed.

As it became darker and darker, the four of us grew more and more quiet, each alone with his thoughts and prayers. The tension had pulled my nerve endings to the surface of my skin to such a point that when Lyle whispered, "This is it, gentlemen. Showtime!" it was all I could do to keep my hands from shaking uncontrollably. I put them in my pants pockets, pretending to be nonchalant as we walked toward the Zodiac. Although appearing relaxed, I was sure the other three could hear my heart exploding like the cannons in the *1812 Overture* as we slipped silently out of the marina toward the stern of *The Circuit Breaker*.

TWENTY-FIVE

Barry and Lyle were on opposite sides of the Zodiac—Lyle in front, Barry in the rear, each with small paddles which barely moved us forward. Both were careful not to slap the paddles or pull them out of the water too quickly for fear of making noises that could alert Granger we were coming. The evening wind blowing across the cool water of the bay was in sharp contrast to the warm summer air which had surrounded us all day long. I wanted to sneeze, but I was afraid to make a noise. I suppressed the urge by rubbing the roof of my mouth with my tongue while I inhaled deeply through my nose.

Rich whispered almost inaudibly, "This is getting spooky, isn't it?"

Lyle gritted his teeth, put a finger to his lips to signal silence, then shot Rich a look of condemnation for speaking.

Rich started to say "sorry," but all he got out was "Sssss . . ." before he caught himself.

I'm sure it only took us minutes to get to *The Circuit Breaker*, but it felt as though hours had passed. It was as if my life was in slow motion except for my heart, which raced at triple time with thumpings I was sure could be heard in the stillness of the starry night. As we reached the stern of *The Circuit Breaker*, I wiped my right hand across my face and was surprised by the moistness of my palm. At first I thought I had put my hand in the bay as we were paddling out, but then I raised the other palm to my face and realized I had broken into a sweat coating every pore of my skin.

Lyle pushed aside Granger's small fiberglass dinghy tethered to a stainless-steel boarding ladder running down the center of the stern. He looked at the four of us, making eye contact to make sure we remembered our instructions, then nodded his head to signal the beginning of the boarding. He reached for the ladder and pulled himself forward in a quick motion. He pushed off of the Zodiac with his right foot to give himself more thrust, but also shoved the three of us away from *The Circuit Breaker's* stern in the process. Barry reached for the ladder, but we had already shot by and had to paddle back again. Lyle stood on the lower rung of the boarding ladder glaring at us as if we had intentionally pushed ourselves away from the boat. He slowly, stealthily inched his way up the ladder until he was standing on the deck. On the port side of the boat he tucked into a tight crouch, a near-fetal position. He was difficult to see even though I knew he was there.

Barry followed by having me hold the ladder for stability so the Zodiac wouldn't be propelled backwards. The way he boarded made holding the ladder seem unnecessary. He stretched himself straight up, arms extended above his head as far as they would go, wrapped his big hands around the rails of the ladder, and pulled himself up as if he were doing a chinning exercise. His legs lifted out of the raft, and he curled them onto the first rung of the ladder. As he stood on the rung, I realized he was wearing the same silly red floral shorts and yellow T-shirt I had teased him about earlier. His jogging shoes made a high-pitched squeak, the kind basketball shoes make on a hardwood court, as his feet hit the deck. I couldn't see Lyle's face, but I knew he was glaring at Barry and would have cursed him loudly except for the required silence.

I was next to go up the ladder, but it seemed impossible for my legs to stretch far enough to reach the first rung. I knew I didn't have the upper-body strength to pull myself up as Barry had done, so I stretched as far as I could and pulled with a mighty heave. My right hand was so wet with perspiration that as I pulled myself upward, my hand slipped from the rail of the cool, stainless-steel ladder. I swung backwards, my left hand still wrapped around the ladder, my left foot balanced gingerly on the lower rung, while my back swung to the stern and slammed into it with a resounding thud. Rich grabbed at me, pulling my right leg so I would be facing forward, so I could get a better grip. I felt the boat rock, then saw a small light from below deck pop itself through the darkness of the night. A growl in the pit of my stomach churned as I knew I had just blown our silent invasion. I clumsily groped for the ladder in an attempt to get aboard.

Someone yelled from inside the boat, "Hey! What's going on there?" I heard some shuffling of feet. I was on the top rung of the ladder when I saw a bare-chested man standing at the door to the cabin area with a pistol pointed squarely at me.

"Who are you? What are you doing here?" he barked.

My throat was so dry, I couldn't have said a word regardless of the threat.

The three gold chains around his neck hung motionless, but the cat's-eye ring on his little finger twitched around the handle of the revolver he was pointing at me. "You've got three seconds to answer, mister, or I'm going to blow you into the water."

He pointed the pistol directly at my head and counted as he stepped toward me. "One . . . two . . . thr . . . ughhhhhhhh . . ."

Granger's gun flew in the air and thudded along the teak deck of the boat. He was doubled over in pain from a kick delivered to his solar plexus. Barry's movements were so sudden, they were as frightening as they were effective. He had jumped into the air to kick the gun out of Granger's hand, landed on one leg, and swung the other squarely into Granger's stomach just below the breastbone.

"Nice going, Gieselmann!" Lyle cheered as Granger groaned loudly.

"What was that?" I asked in amazement.

"Crescent kick followed by a direct kick. I studied Tae Kwan Do for a while." Barry turned to Granger with a low bow from the waist. "Mr. Granger, I am sorry I kicked you. I was taught my first duty is to run, but you made running very difficult." Barry pointed first to me, then to the bay.

Granger was still in pain, but he had managed to stand with a slight crouch, straight enough so his necklaces were flat against his chest. He pressed both hands against the spot where he had been kicked. Staring hard at Barry he groaned painfully, "You're the guy who helped me with the groceries earlier. Found out what you needed so you could rob me, eh?"

"No sir, I have no intention of robbing you," Barry replied.

Looking at Barry and me, he snapped back sarcastically, "The two of you just decided to make a social call, I suppose. Wanted to borrow a cup of sugar? I know what you're after. Don't try to be cute with me."

"He was telling the truth," said Lyle, standing behind Granger and pointing the pistol at him. In his pain Granger was unaware of Lyle's presence. Granger spun around, shocked to hear another voice, and even more startled to be facing Lyle.

"Fortrain?" Granger asked in shocked surprise. "Fortrain, is that you?"

"Since you wouldn't return any of my calls, I thought I'd make a visit you couldn't ignore," Lyle answered.

Granger looked quietly relieved. Defensive and afraid when he faced Barry and me, he turned sarcastic and biting when talking to Lyle. "This isn't exactly the Cadillac style, is it, Fortrain? You and two others attacking me at night?"

"Him and three others," shouted Rich from the Zodiac. "Can I come aboard now, Lyle?"

Granger put a hand over his mouth and chuckled. "This is great, Fortrain. You're a real class act."

"Shut up! Shut up, Donald!" Lyle yelled. His temper flared. The pistol was shaking. At the moment I was afraid Lyle might pull the trigger. The thought crossed my mind that Lyle wanted us to help him kill Granger, that his real motive had nothing to do with learning the truth behind Louise's death.

"Lyle, don't do anything rash," I commanded.

"I'm the one with the gun, Donald, so you'd better watch your mouth," Lyle said menacingly to Granger.

Granger laughed. He had moved from sarcastic to defiant, full of bravado bordering on arrogance, despite being outnumbered. "Fortrain, the safety is still on, and I left the clip down below," he bluffed.

Lyle switched the safety off and checked the handle of the gun. He gritted his teeth, while Granger laughed even harder. "Liar!" Lyle pointed the pistol in the air and pulled the trigger. A red-orange flash exploded from the muzzle with a resounding crack that bounced around the shores of the bay, shattering the peacefulness of the summer's evening. Other boaters tied up inside the marina came out of their boats looking for the source of the noise.

"What was that?" asked a startled Rich as he came up the ladder.

Granger laughed even harder. "Fortrain, you're such a fool. You've always been a fool—you'll always be one."

Lyle had the pistol pointed straight at Granger's chest. "Don't mock me, Donald!" he threatened.

I was certain Lyle was about to pull the trigger. Granger had defied him in front of us.

"Give me the gun," Barry said with his hand extended.

"Shoot me now and there's a whole fleet of people in the marina who will know where the shot came from. You and all three of your buddies will do time. Go ahead, Fortrain, take us all out with one shot." Granger grinned as he twirled the cat's-eye ring on his little finger.

A long, long, pause followed. The gun was still aimed at Granger's chest. Lyle was no longer shaking. His arm was extended, and I saw his chest lift up and down rapidly as he breathed in quick, shallow breaths. Slowly he lowered the gun so the muzzle was pointing toward the deck. "Let's go below, Donald," Lyle said in a quiet voice. "We're going to talk about Louise." He handed the pistol to Barry as he followed Granger down the steps to the living quarters.

I stuck my head in the gangway opening and saw Lyle take a seat at a table. Granger sat on the opposite side. A whiskey bottle, half a lime, and an empty glass were in the center of the table.

Barry, Rich, and I moved to the front of the top deck to give Lyle some privacy. All the hatch windows were pushed up, however, and we could hear what was being said as if we were down below with both of them.

"That was close," Rich whispered . "Did you think Lyle was going to shoot him?"

"We'll never know," Barry answered in a soft voice.

"I'm going to ask him when we get home," Rich said.

I was tempted to say we would still never know for sure, but I checked myself. Instead, I turned to Barry and put a hand on his arm. "Thanks for what you did back there. I think you saved my life."

"And you saved my soul," he nodded.

"I'm not the one who saved you," I corrected.

"Likewise," he responded.

Rich paced along the full length of the deck while Barry and I sat on either side of the bow, our legs dangling over the sides, arms leisurely resting on safety lines drawn between stainless-steel posts. All three of us tried not to hear what was being said below, but Lyle and Granger were loud and argumentative, taunting each other with accusations at a volume impossible to ignore.

Each of Rich's laps produced another question for Barry and me regarding his upcoming marriage. "Do you really think I should go through with it?" Pace, pace, pace. "Do you think she'll let me go out alone sometimes?" Pace, pace, pace. "Do you think I'm too bald? Do you think she'll get tired of me?" Pace, pace, pace. "If marriage is so great, how come so many couples end up divorced?" Pace, pace, pace. "Do you really think I should go through with it? I mean, really? No fooling, do you really?"

Barry managed to fend off most questions by reminding Rich he was an only child whose parents seemed happy, but also a bachelor, never engaged, and thus unqualified to answer. This left the burden of most responses to me. While I was sensitive to Rich's anxiety, giving lengthy replies aboard a commandeered boat we had just occupied after overcoming the armed skipper did not seem the right setting for premarital counseling. I gave standard counseling responses such as, "Uh-huh," "What do you think?" and "You seem concerned about that" to most of Rich's questions. Sometimes I threw in a simple yes or no to sound authoritative. Regardless of the response, Rich continued pacing since there were no easy answers to relieve his anxiety about making a commitment as demanding as marriage.

Barry talked more about his ideas for growing as a Christian when he returned home. He asked about churches, Bible studies, seeking Christian guidance, finding a mentor who could provide him with shepherding when he needed it. The enthusiasm for his new life was infectious, and it reawakened in me an eagerness to serve—an eagerness dormant for the past several months. The stirrings of commitment, faith, a willingness to lead by being a servant were brought to life with each question Barry asked. I had no idea where God was taking me, but I knew at that moment our conversation was part of His plan to renew my spirit, to equip me for a return to service.

As the three of us on deck contemplated our futures, Lyle and Granger revisited their pasts with more emotion and bitterness.

"You killed her!" Lyle shouted.

"She died. I didn't kill her," Granger argued.

"How? How did she die? Tell me! How?"

"I told you before. I've told the police, I've told the Coast Guard, I've told the newspapers. She fell off the back of the boat at night while we were underway. I was down below sleeping. I was only there for half an hour. I was exhausted. When I came on deck she was gone."

"Why did you leave her on deck if it was a rough night?"

"It wasn't a rough night. All the sails were up. We had winds under ten knots. It was a beautiful summer's night, just like tonight. Would you call this rough?"

Lyle avoided an answer. "I've been haunted by her death," he said. "I can't get her out of my mind."

"Too bad you didn't care for her like that when she was alive," Granger sneered.

"Shut your mouth! Just answer the questions. How could she fall off the boat on a calm night?"

"You agree it was a calm night, then?"

"I would agree you're scum. Just answer the question."

Granger's tone changed from sarcastic to reflective. He spoke more slowly, a tone of remorse in his voice. "She had been drinking. I thought she was all right. Apparently she was drunk. She had been wearing a life jacket, but it was on the top deck when I came up."

Lyle's tone didn't change. "That's a lie! She hardly ever drank. She couldn't have been drunk."

Granger let out a low, bitter chuckle. "Married to her all those years and you never knew her at all. The last five years of her life she was drinking all the time."

"Not so! I never saw her . . ."

"Absolutely right. You never saw her. You never saw her drink, you never saw her cry, you never saw her take the kids to school, you never saw her make the bed. You never saw her because you were never there."

"I worked long hours, I admit. But we went out a lot together."

Granger returned to his teasing, cutting tone. "The two of you didn't go out. You went out and she came along. It was always business gatherings where Louise was an accessory, a beautiful, well-dressed woman on your arm. The perfectly coordinated accent piece for any occasion. You talked cars and quotas, zones and promotions, goals and conquest sales. You had it all, she had nothing."

Lyle flared indignantly, "She had everything. Clothes, jewels, cars. There was nothing she didn't have."

"What she wanted she couldn't buy. She wanted your time, but you had sold it to a higher bidder. You needed another plaque on the wall, another trophy in the trophy case, another letter from the head of sales telling you what a marvelous job you had done. Cadillac was her competition, she knew she couldn't win. There's none better."

"Don't give me that, Donald. *You* were my competition. While I was out making a living for my family, you were hustling my wife."

Granger spoke more softly again. His tone was not sorrowful as much as it was the confession of a person who had come to grips with a lesson learned in some painful manner. "I was alone.

BROTHERS FOR LIFE   165

She was alone. For a while I thought I really was your competition. You were everything I wanted to be once upon a time. You were a college boy, smooth on your feet, quick with a joke, met everyone with charm and self-confidence. Me . . . I was a trade schooler who got lucky in business, but never had any of the charm-school manners to really be accepted. When I needed charm, I hired somebody charming to handle the job."

"What's your point, Donald?"

"I thought I knew my shortcomings. I had been married before. I thought I had learned from that one. Louise needed attention, I was willing to give it. She needed time, I could spend it with her. I was sure I could do better than you. But I wasn't fighting you, Fortrain. I was competing with something stronger—a mental photograph of what a marriage should be and how it should be lived out. I was never in the picture, and you always were."

"What are you saying?" asked a quieter Lyle.

"At first I thought it was some kind of class distinction—maybe she was used to hobnobbing with the upper crust, the moneyed group. But I could buy and sell you seven times over. I go to parties you can't even get invited to. I make contributions to the politicians, and they call me on a first-name basis. You can't get anything more than a form letter from them. It wasn't a class thing at all. In fact, she would have been content to live in a bungalow and never go anywhere except to an occasional movie or the kids' plays at school. She had a vision of what her life with you would be like. She never gave it up. It was the center of her every waking moment."

"Granger, you're such a liar."

Granger grunted. "I wish it was a lie. After a year or so, I knew what I was up against. She knew it too. I did a foolish thing by pressing her to level with me. She said she loved me, but in a different way than you. She felt she had messed up her own life and mine along with it. The guilt led her to heavier drinking."

"You're making this up, Granger. It's all . . ."

Granger interrupted Lyle angrily. "Fortrain, do you know what it's like to compete against an image, a mental model of what life and marriage is supposed to be? Worse yet, to know you'll never be in the picture no matter how hard you work at it? Louise had that picture. Maybe we all have them. Our ideas come from someplace, I don't know where. I do know she died not only with too much alcohol in her body, there was too much of Lyle Fortrain in her total system."

"She didn't drink!" Lyle shouted. "You killed her."

Granger remained calm. "There was an autopsy. She had three times the limit to be considered impaired. I've had to live with her death since that night. You're the one who stalked me; now you've got to live with what happened for the rest of your life. We are each condemned to live with our sins 'until death do us part,' Fortrain. You wanted to know—now you can live with it too."

"You're the killer, not me!" Lyle hollered.

Granger remained calm. "If your heart will let you rest thinking so, more power to you."

"What you don't know is that she called me. Told me you had some strange business other than electrical contracting. She was on to something, and you killed her."

Granger spoke even more softly, almost inaudibly. I must admit by this time I was trying to hear what was being said. "Poor, dear Louise . . . She never understood my world. I have many business transactions each day. I deal with union bosses, subcontractors, politicians, architects. I own warehouses, supply stores, and a garage for repairing my vans. It was a whole new world for her, a world she never understood. I was not in corporate America where everybody had their own little function to perform. I had to be involved in everything because it was all on my shoulders. There is no clear line of demarcation when you own you own business. You have hundreds of businesses, not one. Louise never could comprehend that."

"You lie! You've had two years to think about it. You've made this up."

"To the contrary, Fortrain. You are learning the truth and . . ." Granger paused for a moment. It wasn't long, but Lyle was not in a mood to wait as Granger weighed his words.

"And what?" Lyle demanded. "I'm learning the truth and what? Finish the sentence! And what?"

Granger was not about to be rushed. I don't know what he was doing below, although I was tempted to look through the open hatch window. Barry and Rich were stone-still, waiting for Granger to continue with as much anticipation as I. There was a sound like the shuffling of papers. It might have been Granger or Lyle scuffing his feet on the floor or rubbing his hands across the table.

Granger spoke as if reminiscing—a rambling, sometimes halting delivery, making comprehension more difficult. "She was . . . there is a saying about truth . . . yes, 'the truth will set you free.' Strange how some things come back to you in the most unusual ways. The truth will set . . . Anyway, we were on a shakedown cruise out on Lake Michigan three days before she died. The wind stopped in the afternoon. Sheets hung flat on the masts. We were going nowhere. You know what we talked about, Fortrain? World affairs. Me talking about world affairs, that's rich . . . .world affairs . . . So I told her we were like the eastern bloc countries who were free. They had freedom, but weren't going anywhere, just like us. She said something . . . something about freedom . . . She said freedom is a curse. Right. That's what she called it, a curse. At first I thought she had been drinking too heavily, but it wasn't the case. What was it she said? Yes, yes, I remember . . . She said when there is a hostile enemy who keeps you suppressed, there is someone to hate, someone who is evil. But the curse of freedom is that each person is forced to confront the evil within himself, and that is more frightening because there is no escaping, no liberation, only the pain of living with it until death. Do you . . . Anyway, three days later she was dead. Do you understand any of this, Fortrain? You're a college boy. Is that how you guys talk? What difference does it make, right? Now you know the truth, and it is supposed to set you free. But freedom is a curse. We each deal with the evil within us without any hope of escape or liberation. She died. I've had to live with it. Now you must live with it too, Fortrain. Do you have anything else? I'm getting tired. Do you plan to kill me? You and your three friends who stalked me like an animal?"

"We didn't stalk you. We came across you by accident."

"Now who's lying?"

"You can believe it or not. What do I care? We're fraternity brothers. The bald one is getting married soon."

Granger laughed. "Fraternity brothers? Well, boolah boolah. Or whatever it is you boys say."

I heard a loud crash. I believe Lyle smashed the table with his fist. "You kill a woman and you make jokes? What kind of an animal are you?"

"Give it up, Fortrain," counseled Granger. "I went below, and when I came back on deck she was gone. I took a short nap. I was tired. It was four o'clock in the morning. I didn't think I was asleep that long. Her life jacket was on deck, but she was gone. It's as simple as that. It's the truth. And the truth will set you free. Except freedom is a curse, Fortrain. First you are cursed with what you are, now you are cursed with what you know."

"I had nothing to do with her death!" Lyle demanded.

"No more than I did, Fortrain. And no less either."

"I'll kill you! I will!" Lyle screamed. There were scuffling noises, the sound of metal crashing. Barry jumped to his feet followed closely by Rich and me. By the time Rich and I got below deck, Barry had pulled Lyle away from Granger, his arms wrapped around Lyle's chest and arms to prevent him from swinging. Lyle thrashed with his legs in a mad attempt to kick Granger.

"Still being helpful, I see," Granger said to Barry.

"Killer!" Lyle shouted.

"The hour is up, Lyle. Time to go," Barry said.

Lyle tried to pull away, but knew he couldn't overpower Barry. "Killer!" he taunted as he went up the cabin stairs. "You're a killer!" Lyle kept chanting to Granger even as we boarded the Zodiac.

We moved away from *The Circuit Breaker* as Granger stood on the deck of the boat with his arms spread wide, calling out, "You're free to believe what you want. But freedom is a curse, Fortrain. Freedom is a curse you have to deal with." Then he let out a long, low, evil laugh, a laugh which bounced off the water of the bay and followed us all the way to shore.

TWENTY-SIX

We headed the Zodiac to the beach with Granger's laughter still in our ears. Rich and I were on the oars, while Barry stood guard over a ranting Lyle whose temper was clearly out of control. He swore at Barry for pulling him away from Granger. He swore at me for spoiling the silence of the invasion. He swore at Granger for suggesting Lyle shared the responsibility for Louise's death. He swore at Rich for not keeping the Zodiac straight as we headed into the beach's soft sand.

"Give me the gun. I'm going back," Lyle commanded Barry.

Barry raised both hands in the air as he stepped out of the dinghy onto the beach. "Gun? What gun? I don't have a gun."

Lyle was not amused. "Don't play games with me, Gieselmann. I'm not in the mood."

"And I don't have the gun. I left it on the deck of the boat when we came below to hold you back."

"You idiot! He'll just come looking for us now with the gun."

I tried to cool Lyle down by saying, "He won't come after us, Lyle. He's done his damage."

"What damage? You don't think I was listening to a word he said, do you? Those were all lies out there. Did you believe anything he said?"

"Let's say he used some half-truths," I answered.

Lyle wasn't satisfied with my response. "What kind of an

answer is that? What half-truth? He never said a word that wasn't a lie."

"It wasn't *his* words, but what Louise said rings true up to a point. Freedom can be a curse if we each confront the evil within us and think we've got to live with it until death."

"You think I'm evil, Ron? Is that it?" Lyle moved his face to within inches of mine.

"I think we've all sinned, yes. But there is a way . . ."

"In other words you've sided with that slimebag out there," he shouted in my face as he pointed to *The Circuit Breaker*.

"That's not what he meant," Barry said as he pulled at Lyle's arm to move him away from me.

"Get your hands off me, Gieselmann. You two are in this together. You two have always ganged up on me. I didn't do anything wrong, yet you think I'm no better than a cold-blooded killer."

Rich took Lyle's other arm. "C'mon, Lyle. We're brothers. We can work this out."

"These aren't my brothers," Lyle said as he stared at Barry and me.

"Am I your brother, Lyle?" asked Rich, his long forehead wrinkled, eyebrows raised.

Lyle looked at *The Circuit Breaker*, at Rich, then down to his feet. He slowly raised his head, turned from Barry and me, and said quietly to Rich, "Yeah, Rich. We're brothers."

"Brothers for life?" asked Rich in an expectant tone as he wrapped an arm around Lyle's shoulder.

"Brothers for life," Lyle nodded.

"Well then, how about us brothers dragging this monster back to my truck?" Rich said. He pointed to the beached Zodiac at our feet.

"Just you and me, Rich. We don't need those two."

"Come on, Lyle, of course we need them."

"What for?"

"If nothing else, to help us carry this big moose of a raft. It must weigh a ton." Rich winked at Barry and me as if to reassure us he could cool Lyle down.

Lyle became compliant. "All right, Rich. If you say so. You're the boss."

"Well, if I'm the boss let's each grab a corner of this beast and get it back to the Toyota. In case you three forgot, we have company coming tomorrow. It's the grim reaper disguised as my fiancée." Rich was trying to be upbeat, hoping to elevate Lyle's spirits and cool his anger toward Barry and me at the same time.

We lifted the Zodiac, and as we headed toward the Toyota Rich chirped, "Let's all sing the fraternity marching song!" He began with, "We are the brothers who will fight for the right to . . ." But the three of us did not join in, and his voice trailed off, sounding hollow and frail as we trudged through the small park, each consumed with our own thoughts of the past and the future.

We wordlessly walked past park benches, charcoal barbecue stands, and a sagging volleyball net before climbing the grassy slope to the elevated parking lot. The Toyota truck was in the center of the lot flanked by the Cadillac limousine and an old white van with its hood raised.

As we hoisted the Zodiac into the truck bed, a crash shattered the silence. The hood of the van had been slammed shut. We each spun toward the van in shocked surprise. A small person, barely visible in the evening light, stood in front of the van unaware of our presence. "Why me?" the small person said looking up to the sky.

"Myra?" Barry asked.

"Who's there?"

Barry moved toward the van, followed by the three of us several steps behind him. It was indeed Myra, although she was dressed so differently from the first time I had seen her I would not have recognized her on my own. The Gypsy outfit had given way to black leotards with baggy red socks reaching from just below her knees to her ankles. An oversized, white knit fisherman's sweater engulfed her upper body, making her look even smaller and more frail.

She looked relieved to see us, fearing, I suspect, that four men approaching a lone woman at night might mean trouble. She directed her comments to Barry. "I saw the limo but didn't see you guys around. How did you know it was me?"

"The music of your voice," Barry answered. He was not trying to be solicitous, but it was clear to me why he was popular with women. "What are you doing here at this time of night? What time is it by the way?"

"Probably 11 something. Not midnight yet. I'm the choreographer for the next Suttons Bay musical. The playhouse in Traverse City lets us use their theater for rehearsals when the summer stock show finishes. I was supposed to be there at 11 to block out the first act, but it's past this poor old van's bedtime, I guess. It sure doesn't want to go with me."

Rich volunteered to try fix the van. Ten minutes later he rendered a diagnosis of a cracked distributor cap. This translated into no transportation for Myra until the auto parts store opened the next day.

"First the piano player called in sick, and now I won't show. There will be eight unhappy dancers in Traverse City tonight," she moaned.

Lyle had been sitting on the tailgate of the Toyota, far enough away from us to have the privacy he desired, yet close enough to overhear the conversation. He threw the limo keys to Barry. "Take Myra to her rehearsal," he said.

She seemed embarrassed by Lyle's offer. "Oh, Lyle, I wasn't trying to hint at anything. I was just letting off some steam."

Lyle picked up where he left off with Myra the last time he had talked to her. He was patronizing, using broad gestures, talking to her as if he were dealing with a child, not a grown woman. "Of course you weren't. It's just something I want to do for you. Consider it a way of making amends for my gauche behavior toward you earlier."

"I don't want to put Barry to any trouble," she protested.

Lyle didn't wait for Barry to answer. "He won't mind. Besides, if you need a piano player, he can help you out at the rehearsal."

"I don't want to be a burden." She said it in a way that signaled she liked Lyle's idea.

"I'd like a little quiet time myself, so it would be helping me out," Lyle said. He finally asked Barry in an overly polite way if it would be possible for him to accompany Myra and pinch-hit for the piano player. With a shrug of his shoulders Barry agreed.

"You're a dear," Myra cooed as she gave Lyle a hug. "And of course you are too," she added while cuddling Barry's arm.

"I'll ride home with you guys," I said to Rich. "I can sit in the back."

Lyle glared at me. "I said I wanted some quiet time. Go with Barry." His delivery to me was in direct contrast to the way he had talked to Myra.

"I don't think of myself as noisy," I said testily to Lyle.

"You go with Barry. I'll stay with Rich. That way we'll both be happy." He looked at me with cold eyes suggesting I was unwelcome and unwanted.

Barry attempted to smooth things over by glibly joking, "I'll make you a deal, Ron. If you drive us there, I won't ask Myra to put you in the chorus line."

Hurt and bitter, I turned away from Lyle, took the keys from Barry, unlocked the limousine, and fired the engine of the gigantic car. As we pulled out of the lot, I looked at Lyle and Rich in the rearview mirror. Rich was passively standing by the Toyota watching us leave. Lyle had turned his back to us and was looking toward the bay. I pushed the button that raised the glass partition between the driver's seat and the passenger's compartment to allow Barry and Myra some privacy. I also elevated the partition to retreat from an evil and uncaring world, to a place where the Donald Grangers and Lyle Fortrains no longer existed—at least for a while.

TWENTY-SEVEN

One! Two! One, two, three, four!" Myra called out the rhythm beginning each dance number. The dancers went through their routines with an energy and eagerness that disguised the time; it was past one o'clock in the morning, but you would never know it looking at the dancers. I must admit I was captivated by the dancing, the vitality, and the care being put into the production. The dance chorus was comprised of a bank clerk, a farmer's wife, two students, a State of Michigan driver's license examiner, a waitress, a factory worker, and a janitor. Not one among them was a great dancer individually, with the possible exception of Myra. She moved with a free-flowing grace that looked so easy and natural. Despite their lack of professional training, the dancers blended together, complementing each other's strengths so well that most weaknesses were transparent even to a casual observer like me.

Barry dutifully played each song, wincing every so often when he made a mistake, nodding on occasion to acknowledge Myra's signal for a change in tempo. Routines were danced repeatedly until the chorus was familiar with each step. New routines were walked through, then danced through, then repeated at a faster pace. The only grumbling came from dancers who berated themselves for missing a step or were unable to remember their next move. They were amateurs in the best sense of the word, drawn together by love of the theater, expecting nothing more than an appreciative audience for their labors.

While I was fascinated by their work, I couldn't help relating it to my own situation. Their energy made me even more eager to be placed back within a ministry where God could be glorified. I had seen similar enthusiasm within the church by people drawn together by a love for Christ. They were willing to give of themselves with an energy which, when accompanied by the caring concerns of others, resulted in works beyond the combined talent of individual members. The focal point for each member was love; a love given to them freely, a love they hoped to return in some modest fashion. Like the dancers, there was little sophistication needed, only an eager, willing chorus and a leader willing to overcome minor difficulties such as late hours and a recalcitrant van. As Myra walked the dancers through a new number, I prayed God would again place me back in a church where I could exhibit my love for Him in whatever capacity He desired. I was willing to be either the leader or a member of the chorus. The role I was to play was not important to me, but devoting myself to Him was.

As I finished praying, I was struck with a strong sense of conviction because I had still not called my wife. I'm sure God was telling me that getting my marriage back in order was a requirement if I intended to be of service to Him. I hopped out of my seat and headed up the aisle of the vacant theater toward the pay phone in the lobby. I fumbled for change in my pocket when I realized it was almost 2 in the morning. No matter how sincere I might be, Diane would wonder about my sanity if I thought she could hold a meaningful conversation at that hour. I stopped just short of the lobby, took a seat near the back of the theater, and made a mental note to call her first thing the next morning. Little did I know how impossible that would be.

As we turned off the lights and locked the theater doors behind us, we were greeted by a violent downpour. It descended with such velocity that it made loud banging noises on the rooftops of the cars parked along the street. The entire dance troupe, Barry, Myra, and I stayed huddled under the narrow overhang of the theater's roof as rainwater spilled over the gutters and onto the sidewalks like sheets of shredded cellophane. Winds drove the rain in a wild, frenzied fashion so there was no refuge from its soaking power. The temperature had fallen nearly 40 degrees from the blistering afternoon the day before. We crowded together as much for body heat as for defense from the rain. The cold wind and rain sprayed against the dancers, who were still wet with perspiration from the rehearsal. A few who wore towels around their necks to stay warm pulled them over their heads for protection. The females looked like peasant women in babushkas, right down to their hunched-back posture. Curling their shoulders and tucking their heads, they bent over like willow trees to fend off the elements. I felt several people around me shiver as the terror of the rain was trumpeted and spotlighted with thunder and lightning.

Barry yelled above the storm for everyone to stay beneath the overhang as I handed him the keys to the limousine. Still dressed in his red floral shorts, yellow T-shirt, and jogging shoes, he strolled casually away from us as if he were out for a pleasant hike on a spring day. He popped an imaginary umbrella over his head as he walked away and simulated a few dance steps of his own, complete with a leap in the air capped off by a click of his heels. Despite the noise of the storm, I could hear him singing as he danced away. He did a Gene Kelley routine from "Singing in the Rain" as he disappeared around the corner and out of sight.

Moments later the big limousine appeared at the front of the theater. Barry hopped out of the driver's side and opened the front and rear passenger's side doors like a proper and unhurried chauffeur in the grandest fashion. He motioned for the entire troupe to get into the limousine. We sprinted to the car with hunched-over heads, scurrying to the doors as fast as possible, only to wait as we squeezed into the front and rear seats. I laughed as we dashed to the limo. To me, we looked like a parade of jet-propelled snails crashing against a wall as we scampered to the car, only to stack up while the rain washed down our backs.

Barry drove five of the dancers to their cars parked on side streets in the theater district. We took the other three home amidst laughter and jokes about how well-treated community theater dancers were these days, being driven home by a chauffeured limousine service and all. The adrenaline generated at the rehearsal was amplified by the rainstorm and limousine ride. The six of us in the car were acting more like a gang of teenage girls at a slumber party than adults who should have been tired from a full day's activity. We turned on the car radio and found a station playing golden oldies. We sang along to each one, faking the words if we didn't know them. Between songs the disc jockey told us about a cold front moving through the area, producing a severe thunderstorm warning. Each time the announcer said there was a 90 percent chance of rain that evening, Barry cranked the windshield wipers to their full speed so they thrash-thrash-thrashed across the glass as if to applaud the weatherman's accuracy.

When the last dancer was dropped off at her home, we turned toward Suttons Bay. Barry, Myra, and I were in the front seat with the heater blowing full-blast. The windows were fogging over, making visibility very difficult. Myra leaned her head on Barry's shoulder as he drove. I wiped the window glass next to me, unable to see even as far as the bay while we curved up Route 22 at a speed that would not get us in front of our headlights. The long day's activities began to pull on me, as if bags of sand were wrapped around every limb of my body. I sleepily leaned my head against the cool, damp window glass, waking up forty-five minutes later as we pulled into Myra's driveway. She kissed Barry on the cheek and thanked him for all his help. It was clear she would like to see him again, although those words were not spoken. He offered to escort her to the house, but she said it wasn't necessary, slipped out the door on my side of the limo, and dashed through the rain to the front porch. Once inside, she flashed a light off and on to signal good-bye.

The wind had died down, but the rain was still falling as if it was angry with the earth and all objects on it, pounding down big drops which seemed to explode on contact. The air had turned from cool to cold, so being rained upon was more punishing than refreshing. As we headed home, I yearned for the comfort and warmth of a bed which would keep me dry, even if I couldn't be free from the rain's companions of growling thunder and snapping light flashes.

Barry said nothing as we drove to Lyle's house. A smile, perhaps even a smirk, was visible on his face. I didn't know if it was the rehearsal, Myra, or a totally unrelated thought he had, but I did not want to interrupt his pleasure by prying. I saw the smile disappear instantly, however, as we pulled into the driveway at Lyle's place. I wiped the windshield on my side several times to make sure I was focused properly on what was in front of us.

"Oh no," I groaned.

"Maybe it's not as bad as it looks," Barry said hopefully.

TWENTY-EIGHT

The Toyota pickup was in the driveway with the driver's window rolled down. Rich's basketball shoes stuck outside the window area, laces hanging straight down as small beads of water dropped deliberately from the tips like some slow-motion mockery of the rainstorm. It was the same scene I had stumbled on earlier, and I thought I could predict what had taken place. To Barry this was a new setting. He wondered out loud if there had been some foul play involved. I told him what I had found the last time Rich was in this posture. I predicted that our soon-to-be newlywed had returned to a habit previously prevented by Lyle. My guess was that Lyle had become preoccupied with his own problems, and Rich managed to sneak away to pursue self-indulgence.

We sat in the limousine for another minute, hoping the rain would slow down, but it continued a strong, steady pace with no sign of relief. Barry, nearly dry from his earlier "Singing in the Rain" stroll to the car, was not too eager to get wet all over again. I too was less than happy at the prospect of being soaked while trying to drag Rich into the house. We toyed with the idea of letting him sleep in the truck, but worried he might catch pneumonia, making his wedding even more disastrous than if he appeared with a hangover. Finally, when we knew we couldn't delay any longer, we burst out of the dry, comfortable limousine into the cold, wet night.

Barry lifted Rich's legs as he slowly opened the door. When I opened the passenger's door, empty beer cans rolled out of the floor of the cab onto the ground. Additional cans lay littered on the floor; in the center of the mess was an empty pint bottle of whiskey. Rich winced as the domelight glowed through his half-closed eyes. He tucked his legs up to his chest, wrapped his arms around his knees, and mumbled something that sounded like "not a good idea" or "not my idea." He was slurring his words and barely recognized Barry and me. Twice he tried to lay back down to go to sleep in the truck, but we kept pestering him to come in the house, in part for his own good and in part because we were getting soaked to the skin ourselves.

"Rich, we gotta go in, man. My shoes are loading up with water, and I won't be able to walk. Ron can't carry us both," chided Barry.

"'s not a good idea," Rich slurred.

"It's a good idea, Rich," I said, trying to encourage him to move. "You'll catch a death of pneumonia out here."

"Wha' difference it make?" he asked. "I'm a goner eitherway. They're gonna get me one way or theother." He ran his words together, but I really wasn't in a mood to pay attention to what he was saying.

"Sit up, Rich. We gotta go inside, man," Barry continued to prod.

"Gonna make a loud noise. KaBOOM! Scary. Don' like it. Not a good idea."

"It's just raining now. The thunder and lightning have gone away. Come on, Rich. Barry and I'll give you a hand."

He slid toward the driver's side, scooting along inch by inch. I crossed in front of the truck to give Barry a hand so one of us could be on either side of Rich. "Arghhhhh, 's cold outhere," he howled as we held him up with one of us on each side, his arms flopped around our shoulders. Rich was shorter than either Barry or me, and we half walked, half dragged him on the tips of his toes toward the house:

"We've got to get you cleaned up for tomorrow, pal," Barry said as we inched our way up the driveway.

"Makes nodifference. Can' get married anyway. Not a good idea."

"Sure it is, Rich. Marriage is a lot of fun." I no more than had the words out of my mouth before recognizing that my own marriage was no longer a lot of fun, although it had been truly enjoyable not so long ago.

"I tole him, 's not a good idea. Can't get married now."

We were practically to the house. Barry asked if Rich could stand with just my help while he looked for the key beneath a doormat. "Sure, I'mfine. Dumb place to putakey, isn'it? Everybody looks 'ere firs'. But then, Lyle has lotsa dumbideas."

Barry stepped away from Rich. Rich immediately fell into a heap on the front step, almost pulling me over with him. "Come on, come on, Rich, let's get up," I said as I tugged on his arm. Barry opened the door, and together we lifted him into the house.

"Needabeer," Rich groaned as we plopped him into a kitchen chair.

"No more for you, pal," said Barry as he put a kettle of water on the stove. "Tea is the strongest drink you're getting."

I added,"Besides, it looks like you mixed a little whiskey with your beer. That's pure disaster. We've got to get you clean and sober before your fiancée comes. Better take off those wet clothes, Rich. I'll get some dry ones out of your room. I hope I can sneak by Lyle without waking him."

"Not here," Rich burped.

"Not here? Why not here? We won't watch you change if you're shy," Barry mentioned as he dropped a tea bag in a cup.

"Lyle . . . e's nothere. Tole him 'snot good idea to do that either."

"Do what?" I asked.

"Takea ski boat out. Got atop up, but gonna getwet."

The tea kettle began to whistle. "What do you mean, 'not a good idea either'?" Barry asked.

"Huh?"

"You said you told him it was not a good idea either. What does that mean?"

Rich looked at the floor. Puddles of water were forming around his feet. The laces of his shoes were wet and coated with a layer of sand. "I forget," he said unconvincingly.

"Oh no, you don't," challenged Barry.

Rich looked at me for help. "I have blackouts. Tell him, Ron. 'spossible, isn'it?"

"Not this time though, Rich. You do remember," I said as I placed a hand on his shoulder.

Barry placed a cup of tea in front of Rich. He sipped it to keep from talking. Barry was not about to let up, however. "Are you telling us Lyle is out on the bay right now with the weather like this?"

Rich nodded his head up and down, still sipping his tea.

"Fishing?" I asked incredulously.

Rich shook his head sideways, then took another sip.

"Did you start drinking after Lyle left?"

Rich shook his head no again. His face was wet. At first I thought it was from the rain, but I realized he was sweating. Barry spotted it too. Together we grilled Rich since it was clear something was very wrong.

"Rich, something's rotten here. Get it out," Barry ordered.

"I forget. When I drink, I forget sometimes."

"What got you drinking again, Rich? Lyle was keeping a close watch on you."

Rich snickered. "Yeah, he watched me drink from up close all right."

"What does that mean?" Barry's patience for Rich's games was growing thin.

Rich took another sip of tea. The sweat formed in dozens of beads on his forehead, including the expanse of his bald spot. "It means he bought the booze and the beer, and we drank it in my truck."

"What? What for?" Barry shot back.

"So I'd help him use the plastic," Rich said with moist eyes. "I told him it wasn't a good idea. Honest, I did. But he kept insisting." Rich looked like he might cry at any moment.

"It's O.K., Rich. Just take a deep breath, tell us what happened," I said softly.

"I forget. I been drinkin'."

Barry pulled Rich out of his chair by the shirt. With tight fists tugging him up in the air so Rich was on the tips of his toes, Barry shouted into Rich's face, "Stop stalling! You remember! If you don't start talking . . ."

I pulled Barry back. Rich slumped down in the kitchen chair and cried. It was not a sob, but a small, frail, pitiful cry. He spoke as he cried, stopping to wipe his nose with the back of his sleeve. "I didn't want to do it. Honest."

"Just tell us, Rich," I encouraged. "Take a deep breath and tell us what happened." I handed him a Kleenex, and he blew his nose. Another sip of tea and what seemed like an excruciatingly long pause later, he began to talk more clearly.

He took a deep breath, shook his head no, looked at Barry and me, and spoke in a near monotone. His eyes sunk low; he looked tired and beaten. "Right after you two left, Lyle askedme if I wanted a drink. I thought hewas joking. I told him no, I had to begood until after the wedding. He said oneortwo wouldn't hurt. Said he'd buy. I figured if it wouldn't hurt andhe was buying . . ." Rich's voice trailed off. He looked into the black night where the rain continued to pelt everything in sight.

"Go on!" Barry stated firmly but with less intimidation than his last outburst.

"We drank for a while. Had a pint. Couple of six-packs. Lyle talked about the plastic. Could I help him one last time?" Rich took another sip of tea. He was starting to pronounce words as if he were sober, but his train of logic was still difficult to follow.

"What plastic?" pushed Barry.

"KaBOOM! That plastic," Rich fired back testily. "The-stuff-to-blow-open-the-safe plastic. The stuff-I-know-how-to-use-and-he-didn't plastic."

"Oh no!" I moaned.

"We've got to get down to the bank!" Barry barked. "But how

did he get in there? Myra was with us. If he hurt her brother I'll . . ."

"Goin' to the bank won't do anything," Rich said like a teacher correcting a grade-schooler.

"You two didn't go through with the bank idea?" I asked expectantly.

"No. Oh no, no, no."

I exhaled with relief. "Thanks be to God," I said gratefully.

"I wish that's all we had done," Rich said mournfully. He began to cry again, and I didn't think he would ever stop. He put his bald head down on his hands as Barry and I watched his head and shoulders shake with strong, violent convulsions.

TWENTY-NINE

Gravel spit from the rear wheels of the Cadillac. I could hear it clatter against the heavy underbody and rear bumper as I stomped on the accelerator too heavily. The rear of the huge car swung to the right, then back to the left as I overcorrected the steering in a frantic effort to move down the road more rapidly than the limousine's capabilities on a wet gravel road. The rain had turned to a gentle falling mist, so I could use the high beams to light my way. The twisting, turning road had cavernous storm ditches on both sides, yawning wide in a hungry effort to swallow any person or machine making an error along the narrow two lanes allowed for traffic. Huge trees warned me they could smash any car or truck by merely standing firm should I gain enough speed to hurtle the gap made by the ditches.

Several hundred yards ahead of me, the Toyota pickup darted in and out of the bright beams like some flitting firefly. The painted name on the truck's tailgate was caught in one of the Cadillac's beams at isolated moments, so I would see only TOY or YOTA or TO or TA as the truck swung left and right in front of me for a fleeting moment before disappearing into the night's blackness. The Zodiac was strapped into the truck bed, but was being lifted by the air currents beneath it, straining to become airborne, as if it yearned to test its merits as an amphibious vehicle.

Through the rear-window glass above the Zodiac I could make out the heads of Barry and Rich as they lurched from side to side as centrifugal force told them the truck was on the outer limits of the laws of physics. Twice the truck got sideways, so my high beams didn't hit a tailgate but illuminated a truck in profile, its rear wheels spinning in a frenzied rotation to stay pointed straight.

My mind was racing as fast as the speed of the Toyota and Cadillac combined. I knew our situation demanded prayer, yet all I could say was, "Dear God." I repeated the heart petition hundreds of times as we hurtled our way down gravel roads toward the main highway. When I could see the straightaway that would head us onto a paved road, I dropped my headlights to a low beam so as not to blind Barry, the driver. Despite a stop sign where the two roads met, Barry turned a hard right without slowing, the truck fishtailing its way toward the center of town.

I remember thinking it would be wonderful if helpful Officer Timmons was around and would follow either of us as we ran the stop sign. There was no sign of life anywhere, however. Only a few streetlights made dim by the mist suggested humans would sometimes be out at this hour of the morning. We shot by the sign welcoming us to Suttons Bay, home of the 1985, '87 State Girls' Cross-country Champions, across railroad tracks unused in twenty years, and on into the center of town where a few parked cars in front of stores added validity to my earlier notion that this town was the model for plastic villages placed next to electric train sets across America.

Barry pulled another hard right at the green sign with cream-colored letters pointing us to the beach, park, and marina. I followed him; my stomach lifted through some trick of gravity pilots call a G force as the Cadillac gently bounded its way over an asphalt knoll strategically placed to alert drivers they were entering the parking lot. Two seconds earlier the truck had encountered the same knoll and became momentarily airborne, all four wheels off the ground, looking like it had mysteriously hit a trampoline which catapulted it upward and forward at the same time. Barry sped forward toward the boat launch ramp as planned, slamming the brakes to spin the bed of the truck so the Zodiac could be unleashed and dropped into the water immediately. I held my breath as I sped past the front of the truck, cut past the harbor-master's shanty, and headed for the center of the capital W sepa-rating the marina from the beach area. Telephone pole pilings cut three feet tall and spaced only wide enough for pedestrian traffic stood at the base of the peninsula formed by the capital W.

I slammed the accelerator as I approached the pilings. The big bumpers reinforced by the weight of the Cadillac snapped the pil-ings off like toothpicks. The limousine thumped its way along the grassy peninsula, past the boat gas tanks and pump-out station, past two green park benches, and right through a third one which exploded and scattered in the air as the Cadillac splattered any-thing that tried to keep it from its appointed position.

As I got to the tip of the peninsula, the limousine slid to a noise-less stop with front and rear wheels digging into sandy, grassy soil. I flashed the headlight beams to high and pointed the nose of the car forward so the words *The Circuit Breaker* were centered directly above the Cadillac crest on the hood.

"He's out there!" I panted after sprinting back to the boat launch to help Barry and Rich finish unloading the Zodiac.

"It won't matter. We're too late," Rich said sadly.

"How do you know he's there?" Barry asked. "Could you actually see him?"

"Yeah. It's just like Rich said."

"We can't make it, guys. Let's just stay here. My life is over—you don't have to risk yours too." Rich was standing in the water by the boat launch. The mist had soaked him, so the fringes of what little hair he had hung down around his ears. Except for the seriousness of the situation I would have laughed, since he looked like a little friar who had just been baptized.

"What time is it?" Barry asked.

"Almost 3:30. It's no use, Barry. We can't do it." Rich looked and sounded like a child. It was not so much his whining tone as the absence of a belief anything positive could be done that ren-dered him small and helpless.

It was then that so many revelations, so many answers to questions which had gone unanswered for years became clear to me.
I prayed I might live to be able to share that moment punctuated
not so much in words as in a look, a brief stare, an instant which
could never be imitated or duplicated. Barry looked squarely at
Rich. There was no condemnation in the way he looked or the
tone he used when he spoke. There was a compassion, an under-
standing, and at the same time a steely determination, clear and
unmistakable. Barry's eyes, the same eyes that disappeared into
tiny slits whenever he smiled, opened wide, capturing all the light
available near the launch ramp. With a boldness coming from a
source deeper than himself he said, "Rich, stay here if you like.
Ron and I are going out to the boat. When we're finished, we'll
come back to take you home."

Barry said nothing more as I jumped into the Zodiac after him.
We strained on the oars for one or two pulls when Rich called,
"Hold it! I'm coming along." He piled into the Zodiac, hands
shaking, his lower lip pressed beneath his upper teeth. "You two
have turned into more than religious nuts. You're both plain
nuts."

"God didn't put us in this situation to be bystanders, Rich,"
hollered Barry over his shoulder as he dipped an oar in the water
with power and drive.

"Well, you both better be prayin' for all you're worth," Rich
answered back. "We've got less than thirty minutes or it's all
over."

"I've been doing just that from the time you told us what's happening," I yelled to Rich.

"Me too," echoed Barry.

"Holy Mary, Mother of God, blessed art thou among women,
and blessed is the fruit of thy womb, Jesus," Rich mumbled. He
repeated the prayer three more times.

Barry said, "I didn't know you were Catholic, Rich."

"I'm not," he answered. "I'm scared."

The Zodiac refused to move as fast as our arms and bodies
yearned for it to go. We moved out of the channel toward the *The*

Circuit Breaker, anchored far beyond the tip of the peninsula. As we passed the last of the peninsula's landmass, we could see the boat more clearly. The rain had practically stopped, and the Cadillac's high beams were illuminating the stern clearly. The stainless-steel ladder down the center of the stern reflected shafts of light, as if to signal us toward it with some Siren's allure. Almost as if to tease us, the stern of *The Circuit Breaker* swung to the northeast, forcing us to row the Zodiac even further. As my arms throbbed for mercy, a sight loomed in front of us with a shock that was both repelling and frightening. I had seen it from a distance, but the full impact was magnified as we drew closer to *The Circuit Breaker*.

The ketch was outfitted with two masts, a mainmast near the forepart of the boat, and a mizzenmast at the aft. A horizontal boom holding the sails protruded from each mast. The boom of the mainmast was about three to four feet above the deck of the ketch, holding lines and canvas. At the mizzenmast, however, the boom extended four to five feet above the deck, and it had more strapped to it than sailing gear. It had a man lashed to it. His arms were stretched wide as if he had been crucified, except his wrists and arms were tied to the boom instead of being pierced by nails as Jesus' had been. His face was battered. Blood ran out of his mouth and down his body. He was naked except for a pair of white cotton underwear soaked by the rain. The height of the boom was such that he had to stand on the tips of his toes to keep the ropes from cutting his arms, although it was clear some damage had already been done to the muscles above his elbows. As we drew closer, the three gold chains around his neck hung flat and lifeless against his chest.

Donald Granger groaned in agony as we boarded the stern of *The Circuit Breaker*, his eyes glazed in terror. I didn't know which of the three of us, Donald Granger, Rich, or me, was the most afraid of what might happen. The only one who seemed confident we were doing what we were called to do was Barry. He ran to the galley and came back on deck with a long butcher knife in his hand.

"Get below and do whatever you have to do to disarm that thing!" Barry barked as he began to carve away at the ropes binding Granger.

"I'll kill you for this," Granger moaned.

"I don't know if I can do it," Rich cried. His hands were shaking. He looked old and pathetic.

"You'll never do it by standing there shaking! Get below . . . Now!" Barry yelled.

"You're a dead man, Lyle. I'll get you for this," Granger babbled.

"I'm not Lyle, but we're all dead men if we don't get moving," Barry answered as Rich and I went below to the cabin.

Charts, papers, books, and cooking utensils were scattered throughout the cabin. Obviously Lyle and Rich had not subdued Granger without a struggle. A flashlight lay on a cushioned bench beside the table where Lyle and Granger had held their earlier conversation. "Hand me the light," Rich said. When I gave it to him, his hand was shaking so badly I didn't think he could hold it in one hand.

"What do we do, Rich?" I asked out of ignorance.

"First we find the sole plate that covers the keel," he said as he kicked papers and books aside. "I rigged an alarm clock to the plastic explosive. It's set to blow at 4. I mounted it on the through-bolts of the keel. They're covered by a wooden panel here on the floor."

I got down on my hands and knees, pushing aside pots, pans, and papers in an effort to find the panel. "Here it is!" I yelled. A rectangular cover less than three feet long was directly beneath my knees.

"You guys doing all right?" Barry called from above.

"Making progress," I yelled back as I pulled the cover up.

Rich flashed the trembling flashlight into the dark hole. A shallow puddle of water was in the hold, but I couldn't see an alarm clock, wires, or the plastic explosive. "This isn't it," Rich said as his voice quivered. "This is the bilge pump."

"Why didn't you say so?" I snapped back angrily.

"I don't know. They all look alike. It's gonna blow. I'm telling you, we gotta get off of this boat." Rich was immobile, standing there in the cabin with the flashlight in his hand, his whole body shaking with terror.

"Here's another one!" I shouted as I ripped the panel up. This one was the hold for the keel. I could see the metal bar where the bolts were fastened, although I still couldn't see an alarm clock.

From above I heard Barry yell, "I can't cut through all these ropes fast enough. You're going to have to disarm the detonating device."

I could hear a clock, its high-pitched ticks sounding like castanets being shaken by a madman. "I can hear it, but I can't see it!" I yelled to Rich as if he were far away. "Shine your light down here."

Rich got down on his knees and flicked the flashlight around the hold. In the very front, the furthest distance from us, was the clock with thin copper wires coming out of it. I couldn't see the plastic, but it didn't matter because I was so relieved just to see the clock. "There it is, Rich!" I yelled again.

"I see it," he said solemnly. "What time does it show?" He tried to hold the beam of the flashlight on the clock, but he was shaking so hard I couldn't read it.

"Let me hold the light," I said as I took it from him. I found my hand was shaking also, but I was able to steady the light enough to tell it was 3:55. We had less than five minutes until the alarm would ring, detonating the plastic, blowing a hole in the boat, and killing all four of us in a quick, merciless explosion.

From above, Granger babbled over and over again, "I'll get you, Lyle. I'll get you, Lyle. I'll get you, Lyle." The clock's ticking acted like a metronome to his chant.

"What do we do now, Rich?" I said without taking my eyes off the clock.

"I've got to get my hand back there and dismantle it."

"I'm glad you know how," I sighed with relief.

"Who said I know how?"

"You put 'em together, don't you?"

"And they all blew up. I never took one apart before."

Those words did less than give me confidence in the outcome of the situation—much less.

Rich lay on his stomach, reached forward with his right hand, stretching as far as he could. He was trying to steady himself with his left hand, which was shaking so badly I was afraid to imagine what his right hand was doing. He grunted out phrases as he strained to reach the clock. "C'mon, you rotten . . . Can't get my hand around . . . I think it's . . . no . . . Where is the . . ." Finally he pushed himself up with his left hand. I pulled at his arm so he could get to a kneeling position. He looked more frightened than ever.

"Did you get it?" I asked eagerly.

He shook his head. "We're dead. I can't reach it. I put the thing together, but Lyle stuck it back there. His arms are longer. C'mon, we've got to get off this tub now!" Rich dashed through the companionway to the deck with me in close pursuit.

"We're out of here," Rich stated as he headed for the stern.

Granger's left arm dangled freely, but his right remained strapped to the boom. Barry was still carving at the lines with the butcher knife. "I'll kill you, Lyle. I'll kill you," Granger repeated. His eyes were wide-open; the blood from his mouth had dried into a crust around the left side of his upper and lower lip. He looked like a haunted man with hollow eyes and a lifeless expression.

"Hold it!" Barry yelled as he grabbed Rich by the shirt. "I can't get Granger down. We go nowhere without him."

"But we're going to die!" Rich whined.

"Not me. I'm going to live forever. Now, figure out a way to stay alive without leaving this boat."

"Can I dismantle it?" I asked Rich. "Lyle and I are about the same height. I could reach it. You tell me what to do."

"It might work," he said reluctantly. We scampered back to the cabin, where I lay on my stomach, reaching into the hold, awaiting Rich's instructions.

"I just thought of something," he said quickly. "We can buy some time if you can reach around the back of the clock and turn back the time. That will give us a chance to figure something out. That'll work!" he cheered. "Why didn't I think of it earlier? We can do it! It'll save us!"

I stretched my hand as far as it would go. I could feel the face of the clock. The tips of my fingers touched the thin wires protruding from the back. I was startled and frightened by the cold metal scraping against my skin. I pulled my hand back quickly out of fear that merely touching the wires would set off a blast.

"Gonna kill you, Lyle. Gonna kill you, Lyle. Gonna kill you, Lyle," Granger kept chanting, while my heart pounded so hard I could feel it beating through my chest against the floor of the boat.

"I can reach it, Rich. What now?" I said out of the side of my mouth, afraid to even speak too loudly.

"Can you feel the thumbscrew on the rear of the clock?"

I let my three longest fingers delicately caress the back of the clock. "Yes. I've got one. Shouldn't there be two—one for the time and the other for the alarm?"

"There are wires running through the alarm thumbscrew. Can you feel them?"

"Yeah. I touched them before."

"Then the one you're touching is the one that sets the time. You've got to turn it so the hands of the clock reverse."

Rich sounded more calm, more assured now. His earlier panic had been put aside as he talked to me about the clock's mechanism. But I asked one question too many, and he quickly reverted to fear and trembling.

"Rich, how do I know which way to turn the thumbscrew?"

"What do you mean?"

"If I turn it clockwise, will the hands go clockwise or not?"

"How do I know?" he shot back testily.

"Well, you put the thing together."

"I don't remember."

"Rich, sometimes you use that line at the worst times."

"Well, look at the clock and see which way the hands go," he yelled.

"In case you can't tell, I'm flat on my belly with my face pressed against the floor. I can barely reach the clock now. I can't get my head in the opening and reach the clock too. You've got to remember!"

"I don't remember!" he shouted.

"I'm going to kill you, Lyle. I'm going to kill you," Granger groaned.

Rich yelled to the deck, "Barry! Don't you have him free yet?"

"No!"

"Rich, I've got to do something. What should I do?" I implored.

"I don't know, I don't know, I don't know, I don't know," he cried as he sat down on the floor and put his hands over his ears, rocking back and forth. "To the right. No! To the left. No! To the . . . I don't remember! I don't remember! You've got to decide! I can't."

I felt my thumb and forefinger tighten around the thumbscrew. I said a quick prayer and slowly—painfully slowly—turned the thumbscrew as its serrated edges dug into the skin of my fingers.

THIRTY

BBBBBBBBBBBBBBBBBBBBBBBBBBBBBBBBBBBBB
bbbbbbbbbbbbbbbbbbbbbbbbbbbbbbbbbbbbbbb
bbbbbbbbbbbbbbbbbbbbbbbbbbbbbbrrrrrrrrrr
rrrrrrrrrrrrrrrrrrrrrrrrrriiiiiiiiiiiiiiiiiiiiiiiiiiiiiiii
nnnnnnnnnnnnnngggggggggggggggggggggggg!!!!!!!!!!!!!!!!!!!!!!
The alarm clattered for what seemed an eternity. I extended my left arm straight ahead, grabbing some sort of wooden post with my left hand. My right arm was inside the hold, folded upward, and my right hand grabbed some kind of pillow on the upper part of the keel's compartment opening. I kept waiting for the explosion, my face squinted tight, both eyes slammed shut, my neck tucked inside my shoulders for protection.

All the time the alarm rang Rich screamed, "AAAAA AAAAAAAAAAAAAAAaaaaaaaaaaaaaaaaaaaaaaaaaaaaahhhhh hhhhhhhhhhhhhhhhhhhhhhhhhhhhhhhhhhhhhhhhhhhhhhhh hhhhhhhhhh," and kept right on screaming for ten more seconds after the alarm went off. On deck I could hear nothing from Barry, but Granger mumbled intermittently, "I'll kill you, Lyle. I'll kill you."

The alarm stopped ringing, Rich stopped screaming, and Granger even stopped mumbling for the moment. And then it was silent. Stone silent. Eerie silent. Deathly silent. I heard sounds I had never heard before—small waves lapping against the hull of the boat, a diesel truck shifting through the gears in the far distance, a sea gull crying its plaintive call from nowhere in particu-

lar to no one special. There was a rustling sound, like the sound
of a toothless saw trying to cut through a piece of lumber, the
sound of a rat trying to hurry its way across a highly polished
linoleum floor. I lifted my head, one eye opened, to see where this
sound was coming from. I saw Rich rubbing his hands together,
left hand over right, right hand over left, over and over again. His
mouth was wide-open, his tongue hanging down as if he had just
finished a two-mile run. He looked down at me, closed his mouth,
and gulped. "It didn't blow," he said.

"I noticed. But is it going to?" I talked out of the side of my
mouth with one eye open and the other squinted shut.

"Can't. The alarm went off. Don't think so. Possibly it could.
Maybe. I don't know."

"And I thought the Book of Revelation was hard to understand."

"Huh?"

I opened both eyes and began to talk in a more normal fashion. "Can we take a look? I'm afraid to move."

"What's going on down there?" Barry called.

"The plastic didn't explode," Rich answered with a giggle.

"Thank you, Rich. That's very helpful. Could you be a little
more descriptive?"

"I'm trying, I'm trying," he grumbled. "I can't do it all. Besides,
Ron has his fat body in the way of the hold."

"Well, can I move or not?" I asked angrily.

"If you want me to check the hold, you'd better move.
Otherwise, you can continue to do that great imitation of the
Statue of Liberty in the supine position."

"I'll kill you, Lyle. I'll kill you," I heard once again.

"I'm down to the last strand in these ropes. Can one of you
guys come here to give me a hand with Granger?" Barry called
from above.

I tried to move, but my left hand was wrapped around the support leg to the table so tightly that my hand wouldn't unfold at
first. Every muscle in my body seemed locked into position, frozen
by fear. As I started to stand, my right hand clutching the sack on

the upper portion of the hold was the quickest to regain its circulation and flexibility. I used it to wipe my face and dust off my clothes, then went topside to help Barry with Granger. I took a blanket with me to wrap around Granger's shivering body. We now had the opportunity to leave *The Circuit Breaker* if Rich thought there was a still a chance the plastic would detonate. "I'll kill you, Lyle," Granger said to me as I threw the blanket over his shoulders. I got on one side of him while Barry took the other.

From down below we heard Rich chortling, laughing a nervous, high-pitched giggle of tension now released. "Come on down here," he hollered. "This will really knock you out." He was lying on his stomach with the flashlight pointed into the hold. "C'mere, c'mere," he said excitedly. "This is really something. Mr. Lyle Smartypants did it up royal this time."

Barry and I sat Granger on the bench behind the table. We lay on our stomachs next to Rich, trying to look deep into the hold. "I don't see anything so unusual," Barry said. I agreed. We could see the alarm clock, some wires running out of it, and the through-bolts holding the keel in place.

"What do you see?" Rich asked impatiently. "Look closer." I squinted, thinking some miraculous sight would loom before me, but I couldn't make out anything which would even rank as interesting, let alone miraculous. Barry expressed the same sentiment.

"Look beyond the wires. What do you see?" Rich asked, trying to give a hint.

"Water," Barry said. "The keel must leak a little, and water gets in. That can't be unusual in a sailboat though."

Rich sat upright and smiled. "It's probably not. But Mr. Lyle Smartypants wanted to put the alarm and plastic far down on the keel so when it blew the explosive would take out the keel and put a huge hole in the hull too. I was too short to reach that far, so he put it there." Rich smiled as if the puzzle was clear to us.

"Keep going," I urged him.

"Boy, you guys are dense," he sneered. "He put the plastic too far down. When it rained so hard, the keel began to take on more water. Pretty soon the plastic was underwater, and it couldn't explode. Maybe some kinds can, but this stuff has to be kept cool and dry. He wanted to be so smart, but he ended up a dummy." Rich laughed. "He thinks I'm a fool. Well, I'm smart enough to know you can't put an explosive underwater and expect it to work."

"Are you sure that's what happened?" Barry asked skeptically.

"Yeah, I'm sure. Didn't go off when the alarm rang, did it? I'm pretty sure. Well, maybe it can. I don't know."

"I'm going to kill you, Lyle," Granger started chanting again.

"Maybe we'd just better abandon this ship. It's been nothing but trouble since the moment it came into port," I said, anxious to get back to shore in a hurry.

Rich was somehow filled with a new enthusiasm. The thought of Lyle the planner, Lyle the perfectionist who thought of everything, the one person Rich looked up to as a model of intelligence and nerve, making a mistake was too good to ignore. "Hold my legs," he ordered. We did as he said. He stretched himself forward into the hold of the keel, reaching as far as he could. He commanded us to bring him back slowly so he wouldn't disturb the clock or the plastic dangling precariously from the end of several copper wires. As Rich stood up, water dripped from the plastic. He smiled broadly as his speculation had proven to be completely accurate. Sensing our discomfort with the explosive in any state, wet or dry, he disconnected it from the wires, went topside, and threw it overboard.

"Boy did we luck out!" Rich chuckled as he came below.

"It wasn't luck," Barry corrected.

"What was it then?" he laughed.

"An answer to prayer," Barry replied without hesitation.

"Ahhh, you don't believe that, do you? We just happened to hit the casino at the right time. I pretty well had it figured out, but I didn't want you guys to know."

Barry and I simply looked at each other, smiled softly, and shook our heads.

"I'm going to kill you, Lyle," Granger moaned. I looked over at Granger, whose color was coming back. He was still drenched from the rain, but he was sitting up straight. His eyes were clear, although they were not focused on any one of us. He rocked back and forth from the waist in quick, choppy motions, reminding me of old people who spend hours in rocking chairs staring emptily into space.

"Where is Lyle by the way?" Barry asked.

Rich gave Barry a stunned look. "I told you earlier. He's out there somewhere on the bay. He took the ski boat out and is waiting for this tub to explode. He said he wanted the best seat in the world to watch it happen. Don't you remember me telling you that?"

"Sometimes when you drink I don't remember so good," Barry said teasingly but without malice.

Rich puffed out his chest. "Don't worry about it, Barry. After all, we're brothers." He waited for us to chime in with "Brothers for life!" But neither of us said it, and Rich spoke the words alone. They sounded hollow and empty. "So, what now?" he asked cheerily, trying to change the subject.

I was troubled by something that came to me at that moment. "Rich, why do they line the tops of these holds with pillows?"

"What are you talking about?" he asked.

"When the alarm was ringing and I thought the boat was going to blow up, I grabbed this post, and my right hand was squeezing a pillow on top of the hold. I remember because my left hand was so tense I could barely move it, but my right was cushioned by something soft on top of the hold."

"You're goofy," he laughed. "There's no pillows down there. Maybe Granger stores some life jackets down there, but it would be a dumb place to put them. If you ever needed some in a storm or emergency, you couldn't get to them. Let me check it out."

Rich grabbed the flashlight as Barry and I held him by the legs once again. He bent himself at the waist so he could shine the light on the top part of the hold where my hand would have been. "Holy Mary, mother of God," he gasped.

"If you're praying again, remember that stuff doesn't work.

Luck is what matters," Barry teased with a little more bite in his voice this time.

"Pull me up before I throw up! You two aren't going to believe this. Hurry up before I get sick!" he yelled. We did as he asked. When he got up, his face was white, and his hands were shaking once again.

THIRTY-ONE

Barry was next to inspect the ceiling of the hold. We grabbed his legs so he could curl his body upward like Rich had done. He called for us to help him back into the cabin, but unlike Rich he said nothing. Instead, he nodded his head up and down knowingly. My curiosity was at a fever pitch, but it was clear neither Barry nor Rich were going to tell me the solution to the mystery of the hold's contents.

I grabbed the flashlight from Barry's hand and dove headlong into the blackness of the hold, my legs held by Barry and Rich. I could feel the blood rush to my head. The beam from the flashlight became the path for my eyes. I pointed the light toward the ceiling to the place where I thought my right hand had been. But finding the pillow I had grabbed would have been futile because the entire ceiling was covered with them. A fishnet supported by a latticework of bunji cords and duct tape held the pillows in place. They were double-wrapped freezer bags filled with a white, crystalline substance. There were dozens of them, perhaps a hundred or more suspended in the fishnet. I had a suspicion about them, but I needed verification from Rich and Barry. I called for them to pull me up. My head throbbed from the blood that had poured into it while I hung upside-down.

"You lousy scumball!" Rich was shouting at Granger. "I wish the plastic would have gone off now."

I interrupted him by saying, "Rich, I'm not too worldly, no

smarter than the six o'clock news sometimes. Based on what I've seen on television, I'd guess the 'pillows' down there are cocaine."

"Partially correct," Barry said.

"Not cocaine?"

Rich turned away from Granger, but glanced over his shoulder at him with a colder, more chilling look than the bitter rainstorm Granger had survived. "It's cocaine, but not your garden variety. It's crack. Manufactured stuff. Brewed in warehouses or anywhere federal agents don't suspect."

"Are you sure?" I asked. My question was directed to both of them.

Barry nodded. "I saw the stuff among the students I was teaching. That junk is lethal. I had more than one person tell me you're addicted with just one hit."

Rich added, "You'll do anything to get some. It takes your mind and your soul."

I tried to be delicate with the obvious question. "Rich, you don't . . . that is, you haven't . . ."

He spared me from going much further. "No, not me." He hung his head and took several breaths. He kept looking downward as he spoke. "My kid brother. Two years ago in Los Angeles. I knew he was smoking marijuana. I didn't see him too much, but every time we got together he was getting high. I suspicioned he had gone to harder stuff, but I didn't want to talk about it. After all, who was I to criticize? One summer night he and another guy tried to rob a liquor store. Had to get money for a crack habit. Store owner had a shotgun under the counter, shot my brother and the other guy. Killed my brother. The other guy lived, but he'll spend a long time in prison. Told me about it. My brother was doing five, six hits a day. Wanted to quit but couldn't." Rich lifted his head. His eyes were moist. "We all want to quit but can't."

"I'm sorry, Rich . . . I didn't know." I was at a loss to say anything more helpful. The depth of his tragedy was on his face, and I knew nothing beyond God's grace that could help him at that moment.

Rich shook his head as if to clear it. "Remember what Granger said Louise told him the night she died? Said something like freedom is a curse because you're forced to deal with the evil inside you instead of the enemy on the outside. She was right, guys. It's exactly what I'm dealing with." He pointed at Granger. "Two years ago I would have said this idiot here was the cause of all our troubles. But my brother, Granger, and me . . . we're all the same. We're all evil. There is no hope for us. We don't need any enemies. We've got ourselves."

"Rich, we can get you some help," I suggested.

"My brother's a dead man. Granger's a dead man. I'm a dead man. The only help you can get us is making sure we have proper burials."

Barry put a hand on Rich's arm. "How about if we clean up the mess one person at a time? Let's get back to shore and get the authorities out here. There's enough stuff on this boat to put Granger away for quite some time."

Rich nodded. "I'll bet there's more too." He violently turned over cushions in the settees, opened cupboards in the galley, tore into the head, overturned the mattresses in the berths. He pried open a trapdoor constructed beneath a berth. There lay another cache of the freezer bags filled with white crystals.

Triumphantly holding a bag in each hand, Rich became excited about the future of Donald Granger. "I'll bet he had something to do with killing Louise too. I can hardly wait to tell Lyle."

"And when we get done with Granger, we'll get you some help too. Right?"

"Do you really think there's any hope for me?" he asked expectantly.

"There's hope for all of us, Rich," I said with authority.

"What makes you so sure I can change?" he asked.

"Because *I* have. And what I was dealing with was much stronger than the alcohol that influences you."

"Were you on dope?" he asked in disbelief.

"No, but I sure acted like one. I'll tell you about it later. For now let's figure a way to get us off this boat. Nothing good seems to happen here."

We wrapped Granger's shivering body in blankets, then put him in an aft-cabin berth. He was still glassy-eyed and incoherent, although he no longer mumbled, "I'm going to kill you, Lyle." It was difficult to understand what he was trying to say since it was a mixture of babble and shivering. Although he was unable to pilot *The Circuit Breaker*, we made sure he would stay put by jamming the door to his stateroom so he was locked inside. The keys to the boat's ignition hung conveniently near the wheel in the pilothouse. Rich put them in his pocket as Barry and I each took a bag of crack to show the police.

The rain had stopped, but the morning air remained chilly. A northeast wind drove the cold air at us with a bitter intensity as we stood on deck. Rich and I shivered as the cold air hit us. Barry's shoulders, arms and legs shook; the silly red floral shorts and yellow T-shirt he wore provided no protection from the wind.

Rich chided, "Barry, put on some clothes or you'll catch pneumonia and die."

Barry's teeth chattered. "I'd like to," he said.

"Die?" asked Rich wryly.

"I told you, I'm going to live forever," Barry said with a quivering jaw.

"There's clothes down below. When Lyle and I were here earlier, we found two seabags filled with clothes. In fact, Granger was wearing a cozy, bright yellow jacket with a hood when we . . . that is, before we . . . you know what I mean. We tossed it in one of the front berths. I don't think Granger would mind if you borrow some clothes until we get back. In fact, let me check with him first." Rich stuck his head in the companionway and said with a mock English accent, "I say, Donald, old chap, do you have any objections to Barry borrowing some of your clothes until the authorities come to lock you away? Oh, jolly good. Well, cheerio and good-bye." He paused, turned to Barry, and said, "He has no objections."

We all went below again to get some clothes for Barry. Granger's pants were easily three inches too short for him. It gave us a good laugh. The long day, the release of tension, and the excitement of turning a drug dealer over to the authorities was making me giddy. Rich and Barry seemed to be affected the same way. When Barry pulled on a sweater which didn't cover his belly button we nearly went into hysterics. The finale to his comedy routine was putting on Granger's bright yellow, foul-weather gear jacket. He flipped the hood over his head and did an imitation of the wolf in "Little Red Riding Hood." None of this sounds amusing today, but at the time the three of us thought it was the funniest act since Milton Berle got hit in the face with a giant powderpuff.

Granger mumbled something from the confines of his stateroom.

"Ah, go soak your head!" Rich hollered.

"He already has," I said. We broke up laughing again.

Granger stopped mumbling as we exited the cabin area. We stood on deck surveying the blackness of the night, noting the boats in the marina, the tranquillity of the beach, and the serenity of a scene whose allure could have served as inspiration for an artist's night seascape. In spite of the quiet, calming effect the scene had on each of us, I had an uneasiness about our surroundings I couldn't identify. At first I thought of ignoring it, but I mentioned it to the other two. When Barry said he had the same feeling, I was more anxious than ever.

"I got it. I know what's bugging you two," Rich said with authority. "Look at the peninsula. What's wrong with that picture?"

I couldn't figure out what he was hinting at. Barry caught it, though. "The lights on the Cadillac are out," he said.

"How long have we been out here?" I asked.

Rich touched a button on his watch, backlighting the face so he could tell the time. "It's past 6. We probably killed the battery."

I accepted his explanation as we made our way down the stainless-steel ladder into the Zodiac. But in my heart I didn't think that's what was troubling me. I wish I would have paid more attention to my heart then. I've since learned to listen to it more often and more carefully, for if the heart is captured, the rest of the body must follow.

THIRTY-TWO

The oars dipped into the bay with soft splashes, stirring the water beside the Zodiac in a smooth, steady rhythm that sounded like gentle waves spilling against the sandy shore. We seemed to be in no particular hurry. The events of the hot day and long night had finally caught up with us, sucking energy from our bodies, draining us of physical power to move the big dinghy toward shore any faster. Even though my body was yearning for a long rest in a comfortable bed, my mind was speeding its way through the events of the day.

The quiet, undisturbed setting of the marina, peninsula, and beach ahead of us provided a calming effect as the sounds around me released the tension of the last twenty-four hours. I heard bird sounds—a loon, its cry clear and lonely, a plea for its mate to return. Small birds, perhaps chickadees, flittered around the distant shore, their playful chirps celebrating the coming of dawn and the company they gave one another. From the boat launch I heard doors slam as fishermen readied a skiff for a pre-dawn launch, their words indistinguishable, but clearly conveying the confidence of knowing how to do their tasks mixed with the hope of being successful. A sporadic clang-clang-clanging of loose lines against the metal masts of sailboats in the marina made a discordant, out-of-sync percussion played against the steady, soft splashes made by our oars. It was all so marvelously peaceful. I would have been willing to simply sit there for fifteen minutes

until the sun rose just to listen to the symphony being played by
God's orchestra.

From the bay itself there was a sound unlike any other. It was
a strong, growling, powerful sound, a whirling which seemed to
get louder and louder. In a matter of minutes the sound smoth-
ered all other sounds in the area as if it were jealous of all noises
but its own. We stopped rowing in order to determine the source
of the noise. We looked to our left and right, forward and backward, but saw nothing. Its noise grew second by second. I remembered that sounds could be heard from great distances on the
water, but the mystery of this sound's origin was heightened by
the crescendo it made as it came closer and closer.

Barry raised his arm and pointed off to our left at about a ten
o'clock position. "There it is," he said quickly and softly.

At first Rich and I saw nothing, but then it was visible. Lights—
two lights. A red/green lens like two Christmas tree bulbs next to
one another formed the first light; the second was a white light,
larger, brighter, and higher than the red/green one. The lights grew
in size as the sound grew stronger and stronger. We each knew the
source of the sound now, but refused to state it aloud, unsure of
what to say or do after the identification had been made. Finally
Rich said what we knew to be true. "It's Lyle in the ski boat. He
must have the engine wide-open."

"He's headed straight for *The Circuit Breaker*," I groaned. "He
looks like he's going to ram it."

Rich added, "He must have been waiting out there for
Granger's boat to blow. Now he's going to make it happen."

"I don't think so," Barry responded. "He's smart enough to
know if it hasn't blown by now there's a defect somewhere."

The ski boat continued its steady, droning roar on a direct path
toward the anchored ketch. Its lights grew larger and larger as its
noise grew louder and louder. I couldn't see Lyle in the boat, but
within twenty seconds the details of the boat became clearer. The
canvas top he used to keep the rain off his head was still up.
Unable to see Lyle driving the boat gave it the appearance of a
phantom craft on its course without a pilot. For a fleeting moment

I entertained the idea that somehow Lyle was directing the ski boat through some radio-controlled device while he stood safely on shore. I wanted the ski boat to be a toy. I wanted this whole scene to be a bad dream, a result of spicy food before going to sleep one evening. But the noise level of the ski boat let me know I was wide-awake with a very live crisis at hand. The ski boat was less than a hundred feet from the stern of the ketch now, bearing down with an ear-splitting intensity. I clenched my fists tightly in anticipation of the crash.

"He's going to ram it!" Rich shouted.

The words were barely out of his mouth when the engine cut back to idle, and the boat glided innocently to a slow speed, propelled more by the wake pushing it from behind than by the drive of the propeller. The ski boat swung sideways at the stern of *The Circuit Breaker* as Lyle grabbed the stainless-steel ladder with one hand, then pushed the ski boat away with both feet as he boarded the ketch.

Slivers of light began to break over the horizon as dawn started its slow rise. The ketch was east of us, so we saw Lyle more as a backlighted silhouette, the details of his features unclear although his movements were easy to identify. He stood on the deck of the ketch for a moment, slicked his hair back with both hands, then put both arms behind him as if he were stuffing a shirttail back into his trousers.

"Oh no," Rich said, "I forgot he took Granger's gun with him."

"Do you think he would . . ."

Rich interrupted me with, "I know he would."

"But we locked Granger up. He could be safe," I said with more hope than assurance.

"He could start mumbling again," Barry argued.

"We've got to stop him," I urged without a clue as to how we could do it.

"Call to him, Rich," Barry said without a trace of anxiety in his voice.

"Lyle! Lyle!" Rich shouted at the top of his lungs.

Lyle turned a full circle trying to locate us. "Where are you?" he shouted back over the stern.

"Over to your left a little. West of you," Rich shouted.

"Stall him for a while," Barry whispered to Rich.

"I can't see you," Lyle shouted back.

"Just stand there for a while," Rich hollered. "Let the sun come up a little more and you'll see us."

"Don't have much time, Rich," Lyle said. "There's something I've got to do."

"Lyle, please don't. Let us come get you."

"Too late, too late. What went wrong, Rich?"

"Please, Lyle. Just stay there."

"What went wrong, Rich?"

"It was the plastic. The plastic got wet, Lyle."

"But what went wrong, Rich? We had it all going our way one time. What went wrong? Where did we miss it? What didn't we do right? It all seemed so right at one time. Why did she do it, Rich? I tried. I really did. I tried with everything I had." Lyle's voice was quivering. He held the gun in his right hand. His shoulders were slumped forward as if he were carrying a bag of sand on them.

A ribbon of orange-red light threaded its way across the horizon. It was just enough light so Lyle would be able to see us.

"Keep him talking," Barry whispered again.

I looked behind me, people were beginning to stir around the marina. A few were pointing out our way, seemingly unhappy with the noise being made at this early hour of the morning.

"Lyle, we need to get you back home. You're my best man at the wedding."

"Sorry, Rich," he shouted. "Looks like I might be detained. Better start it without me."

"Stand up so he can see you," Barry whispered to Rich.

Although the Zodiac had a rigid floor, it was difficult for Rich to stand. The dinghy rocked back and forth uneasily. As Rich got to his feet, Barry slid down in the dinghy, his stomach on the floor, completely out of sight.

"What are you doing?" Rich asked, just as confused as I.

"Keep him talking," Barry whispered back.

"Lyle? Can you see me now, Lyle?"

"Yeah, I can see you. Who's with you? Looks like Ron. Good thing. He can administer the last rites. Or can he do those things? Doesn't matter."

"It's me, Lyle. Let us come get you," I called out.

"Rich, you were always my buddy. We were brothers. Brothers for life. Trouble is, nobody told us what life was all about. But tonight I finally got it figured: If you can't get ahead, at least get even."

"Please, Lyle. Ron and I can help. Let us help you, Lyle."

"I lost Louise, I lost the kids, I'm never going to be a Zone Manager. I've lost so much, the only thing I can do is get even."

"We're coming out there, Lyle. Just stay put," Rich said with as much pleading as authority in his voice.

"Hey, Rich, if you ever go to Las Vegas, remember what I've told you tonight. If you can't get ahead, at least get even. Life isn't meant for losers." Lyle stood up straighter, his shoulders square, chin up. He lifted the gun toward his face. I was sure he was going to put the gun in his mouth, but instead he kissed the barrel and stroked it like a little kitten. "Gotta go, Rich. This little charmer and I got a date. You might say we're going to give it one last shot at getting even." He laughed a strange, evil, demented cackle sounding unlike anything I had ever heard Lyle do before. "Hey, Rich? I'm getting pretty witty up here. One last shot at getting even? That was all right, wasn't it?" Without waiting for a reply from Rich or me, he made his way toward the stairway leading to the cabin area.

"Lyle, you can't!" I shouted.

He merely looked my way. I couldn't see his features clearly, but I think he was smiling at me. "All my life people have been telling me what I can't do. All you got to do in life is think positive, Ron. If you think you can do something, you can. So I think it's time for me to go."

From the floor of the Zodiac Barry howled, "Freedom is a

curse, Fortrain." Barry's voice had the timbre and rhythm of Granger's. He let out a long, low, sardonic laugh exactly like the one Granger had laughed at us the night before.

"Who's that? Do you have Granger there?" Lyle yelled frantically as he jumped up the stairs and pressed against a safety line at the ship's gunwale. He stared at the Zodiac shouting, "You've got Granger, don't you?"

Barry pulled at the top of Rich's pants just above the small of his back forcing Rich to sit down in the Zodiac with a thud. Barry got on his knees, the hood to the bright yellow, foul-weather jacket covering his forehead and eyes. His arms were stretched wide as he continued to imitate the wicked laugh of Donald Granger. "Freedom is a curse, Fortrain," he bellowed as he got to his feet.

"You! You! YOU'LL DIE!" Lyle screamed as he raised the gun and fired off two quick rounds.

Water spit up on our left as the bullets missed their target. Lyle fired again. This time the bullet landed in front of the Zodiac, and we were splashed by its impact when it hit the water. Barry remained standing, his arms opened wide, mimicking the maniacal laugh Granger had used to taunt us.

Lyle fired again.

Rich moved beside Barry. "Lyle, stop it! Stop it! We're all brothers!" he screamed.

"Traitors! Traitors for life!" Lyle yelled back and fired once more.

A loud thud was followed by the Zodiac being swung instantly sideways. Rich fell overboard as the flotation tube on the right side blew air out of a hole created by the bullet. Barry was jolted sideways, but caught his balance and stayed inside the dinghy. He stopped his imitation of Granger and looked for Rich.

Rich broke the surface of the water as another bullet plunked within yards of his head. "I can't swim," he called out in desperation. Barry immediately peeled off the foul-weather jacket, pants and jogging shoes. He was back to the red floral shorts and yellow T-shirt. He dove into the cold bay as another bullet struck the water behind him.

Rich kicked and screamed in anguish as the panic of drowning overtook him. "Help! I'm drowning. Help!" he screamed in terror despite Barry's attempts to calm him.

"Don't fight me," Barry pleaded. I tried to get the sinking Zodiac closer to them. A shot plunked in the water as Barry wrestled with Rich and grabbed the dinghy simultaneously. Lyle fired another shot. Rich went limp. Barry groaned, releasing a long, soft exhale of anguish and desperation. He rolled Rich on his back. I rowed the Zodiac toward the beach as quickly as my arms and the deflating vessel would let me. Barry hung to the back of the dinghy with his right arm, cradling Rich beneath the chin with his left. He kicked to help push us toward the beach.

Lyle fired two more shots but we were beyond his range. With those two rounds fired, his gun was empty. I heard him curse as he threw the gun into the water.

Frightened people in the marina who witnessed the scene had called for assistance. In the distance I could hear the approaching wails of police sirens and ambulances.

"Hang on, hang on," I hollered. "We're going to get there. Help is on the way, Rich. Hang on, buddy. Hang on!"

We reached the sandy shores of the beach. Rich was blue, but I saw no evidence of a bullet wound anywhere on his body as I pulled him ashore. I waved frantically to an ambulance as it searched for us. When its headlights flashed in our direction, I turned around to look at Barry and Rich. Rich was lying on his back, stiff and immobile. His eyes were open, but they stared straight up at a morning sky he couldn't see. Barry walked toward me very slowly. He too had a strange, faraway look in his eyes. He blinked once and fell down at my feet, just as he had done at the airport and in the park.

Except at those times he was pretending.

At those times he rolled over with a big grin to let me know he was only fooling.

At those times he got up and walked away.

At those times death was a joke.

But I was sure this was not one of those times.

THIRTY-THREE

Rich died on the way to the hospital despite valiant attempts by two emergency medical technicians to keep him alive. His fiancée arrived that afternoon thinking she was meeting Rich to apply for a marriage license. Instead, she was involved in making arrangements for his funeral, including the complicated process of having him returned to California. She told me Rich had a heart condition he refused to do anything about. Drinking made his medical condition worse, yet he drank to forget his medical condition. And so he found himself on a perpetual downward spiral ending in the cold waters of Grand Traverse Bay one chilly summer morning.

The official medical report listed his cause of death as a severe coronary infarction, or some such medical jargon meaning a heart attack. I suppose it is unscientific today to suggest someone can die of a broken heart. Broken hearts seem to be reserved for people in poems and love stories. While I will grant you Rich's heart may have been weakened by food, drink, or some hereditary disease, I am convinced it was broken that morning no matter what was stated on the coroner's report, for Rich's story was a love story with an unhappy ending. His devotion to Lyle was unbounded by time or location, for Lyle was everything Rich hoped to be—courageous, ambitious, nervy, creative, and successful. And Rich's story is a love story not unlike most love stories ending in tragedy because he saw only what he needed to see in Lyle, and not what existed in reality.

Perhaps that is the way for all of us, and it is only God's grace that pulls us through when the full reality of the other person becomes apparent. Perhaps we refuse to see the totality of the other because we can only see it if it exists in us too. And such awareness is too frightening without the love of Christ to transport us above that plane. For confronting our own evil is not possible without Him. We may disguise it by saying we are inherently good, or a victim of our circumstances, or a number of other convenient, acceptable self-deceptions. But until we have dealt with the evil within us, we will be unable to forgive it in others. And when the moment of self-confrontation comes, it is only through God's mercy that we will survive.

If you think I am being critical of Rich, you misunderstand. My own cowardice at sharing the gospel with him, my prideful fear of being rejected, my tender feelings which took precedence over impressing upon him what God could do in his life, has haunted me to this day. It took his death to bring me to life. I chose to share Christ with Barry, a companion who would listen and not reject me. And my own personal acceptance took priority, not the message of salvation.

Beyond confronting Rich's death, one of the most difficult tasks I have ever done was to think about comments to make about Barry's life. I wrote some notes I keep yet today in my Bible. I began the document you are reading by saying that next to Jesus Christ I thought of Barry Gieselmann as the most gifted and talented person who ever walked the face of this earth. I am somewhat afraid to make such a statement, however, because unless you knew Barry as I have known him, it sounds as if I am putting him on the same level with our Lord and Savior. That would not be what Barry wanted.

I also had a version extolling his abilities as a musician and athlete—how he nearly made the Olympic bicycle team except for a wrong turn. I didn't like that version either; I was afraid it sounded as if Barry's life could be characterized in "what might have been" except for one wrong turn. Barry had made more than one wrong turn in his life, yet he acted heroically. To mention what he did not accomplish in life would not diminish his heroism, but it would not accurately portray the range of his achievements either.

I believe the most meaningful comments were the ones I planned to tell about Barry's love of Jesus, how he had so many ideas, so much energy, so much enthusiasm for spreading God's Word. How despite his infancy as a Christian he had translated his faith into works, how the Holy Spirit was so alive within him he could do no less than what God would desire of him. I recalled how the night we decided to head out to *The Circuit Breaker* he had a look on his face which unhinged one of my personal mysteries about God's Word. As Abraham and Isaac climbed Mount Moriah for what had to be the sacrifice of the son, I wondered how the servants could be so passive during a time that would obviously involve the killing of another human. Forget that they were servants and were to do as they were told. Forget that Abraham says, "I and the lad will go yonder and worship, and come again to you." Those answers never satisfied my soul. In like manner, I could never account for the cowardice of those who stood by while Christ bore the cross up to Golgotha. But Barry Gieselmann unlocked the puzzle for me. That night, standing in the boat launch with his eyes opened wide, I saw obedience to the command of God, the faith-step required by each of us in spite of the circumstances at hand.

And I remember how I felt that evening, how Rich said aloud what I also thought—it was too late for anything to be done. It was Barry's response through the look in his eyes that told me that as long as we have a God as great as the one we serve, there is nothing impossible if He has blessed it. The fear felt by those who did not defend Christ was no different, no greater, no less than the fear I experienced that night. And it was the evil within me that caused me to doubt. And it was through the eyes of Barry Gieselmann, a messenger sent to me by a loving God, that I came to grips with what would be required of me before I could return to serve Him.

Diane was able to get a leave of absence from her job. We spent three months in prayer, and I thanked God daily for the blessing of a Christian wife who was willing to stand by me, who believed the wedding vows we shared, and who gave me comfort through her strength.

And so I am applying to you now as a candidate for the pastoral opening you have. I am not without my flaws, not beyond the need for your daily prayers. But I have come to know the Lord in a deeper and more meaningful way, a way I hope to transfer to all who would come in contact with me. I realize I have given you more than what you have asked in regard to how I know I have been called to His service. But I felt it was important to explain the entire story so you would understand the depth of my commitment.

Should you decide to hire me, I could arrange at some future date to have a concert of Christian music played by Barry Gieselmann. While I had given thought to describing Barry at his funeral, prayers for God's will in Barry's life were answered by sparing his life on earth.

The doctors were amazed at how a bullet could pierce so close to his heart but not kill him. They attributed it to his extraordinary physical power as a result of years of bicycling. There was extraordinary power involved, but you and I know it extends far beyond his physical conditioning.

Sometime Barry, like all of us, will die.

Sometime Barry, like fewer of us, will enter the gates of Heaven.

God knows exactly when that time will be, but it was not yet one of those times.

THIRTY-FOUR

O f course the person who needed me most was Lyle. He made it clear on a number of occasions that he was capable of climbing above any dilemma in life through the use of his own talent, creativity, and energy. For him, God was not necessary. And for me, loving Lyle was not easy. Yet he was the one among us most in need of love. A mentor of mine was fond of saying, if Christians only love those who love us in return, how are we any different than the rest of the world?

I visited Lyle once while he was in jail. Barry refused to press charges against him. The state was willing to drop formal charges provided Lyle would submit to a psychiatric evaluation and be willing to report regularly to a probation officer. Since that time, I have only been able to talk to him once more on the telephone. I have left many messages, but Lyle does not return my calls. His secretary in the Washington, D.C. zone office tells me Lyle is very busy and is working many long hours. She said he has been given a special project of coordinating an equestrian jump show in Virginia in addition to his duties as Assistant Zone Manager. Two months ago I began to write the newsletter Rich authored, except I send copies only to Barry and Lyle. I close each letter by saying I am praying for both of them daily. I make a pencil note on Lyle's copy telling him I pray specifically for his salvation, and I offer any help to him should he need it.

Lyle was not pursued by the state because Granger was a much more interesting prospect for them. Shortly after being arraigned on drug charges, Granger was out on bail. I understand his lawyer has shown that the local police seized his boat without a proper warrant, so all evidence against him has been quashed. Federal authorities are said to be watching him very closely, and the IRS is investigating his tax returns from the past five years.

I also pray daily for Donald Granger.

As I also pray daily for our nation.